.45-CALIBER
FURY

This Large Print Book carries the
Seal of Approval of N.A.V.H.

.45-CALIBER FURY

PETER BRANDVOLD

Thorndike Press • Waterville, Maine

Published in 2006 by arrangement with The Berkley Publishing Group, a division of Penguin Group (USA) Inc.

Thorndike Press® Large Print Western.

The tree indicium is a trademark of Thorndike Press.

The text of this Large Print edition is unabridged. Other aspects of the book may vary from the original edition.

Set in 16 pt. Plantin.

Printed in the United States on permanent paper.

Library of Congress Cataloging-in-Publication Data

Brandvold, Peter.
    .45-caliber fury / by Peter Brandvold.
      p. cm. — (Thorndike Press large print Westerns)
    ISBN 0-7862-8796-9 (lg. print : hc : alk. paper)
    1. Large type books. I. Title. II. Title: Forty-five caliber fury. III. Series: Thorndike Press large print Western series.
PS3552.R3236A6146 2006
  813'.6—dc22
                                      2006009783

For Carl and Kathy.

1

The man in the funnel-brimmed hat with silver conchos had two white, dime-sized scars on his face, where a drunk Texan had skewered him with a hot poker during a long winter in a secluded line shack.

The poker had gone into one cheek, through Page Hudson's mouth, and out the other cheek and into the shack's floor. Hudson had been pinned to the floor until he'd worked the poker out of the puncheons. When he finally did, and had eased the poker out of his mouth, he used the iron rod to beat the Texan to a bloody pulp.

The Texan had died three days later, and Hudson had dragged his battered body out in the snow, leaving it near the privy for the porcupines and wolves.

Page Hudson was thinking about the Texan he'd killed as he rubbed the knotted scars on his cheeks with his thumb and index finger and stared at the manager of the Brickson & Dodge overnight stage station. The manager stood on the cabin's rotting wood stoop, a hairy hand shading his eyes from the mid-afternoon sun as he stared up at the six mounted riders before him. Stoop-shouldered, he wore shabby coveralls and a shaggy longhorn mustache with waxed ends. The mustache was the manager's ineffectual attempt at hiding a prominent overbite.

The Texan had had an overbite nearly identical to the station manager's. After a couple months in the hip-deep Montana snow, that overbite had become the only thing Page Hudson could see or think about, and he'd gradually become consumed with an overwhelming urge to fix it with a pistol butt.

Now someone nudged Hudson's right elbow, and Hudson turned to see Burt Snyder glowering at him. "Well?" Snyder asked.

"Well what?"

"The man says he hasn't heard of a Massey around here, Page," Synder said, his voice sharp with impatience. "What we gonna do now?"

Nudged from his reverie, Hudson leaned over his saddle horn and regarded the station agent skeptically. "What the hell you mean, you never heard of Massey? We were told in town that Cuno Massey farms out here along one of these creeks. I didn't realize how many creeks there were or I woulda had the gent draw me a map."

The station agent frowned, canted his head, and scratched his scalp. "Well, if there's a Massey out here, I don't know him. Massey, huh?" He shook his head. "No, sir, I never heard o' no Massey."

Hudson stared at the man skeptically. When he and his five companions had ridden into the yard, they'd seen a girl fetching water from the well pump. When she'd seen the strangers, she'd hurried into the cabin, and then the manager had come out.

Now Hudson said, "Send the girl out here."

The station manager flushed, rubbed his hands on his greasy coveralls nervously. "Huh?"

"You heard me."

"She don't know no Massey."

"How do you know?" asked the redhead, Dusty Dale Winget. "You ever ask her?"

Hudson grinned at the station manager's discomfort. The manager flushed and swallowed and shuttled his glance down the line of dusty, well-armed riders regarding him angrily.

Hudson put his hand on the butt of his big

Remington and said, "Send her out here."

Still, the manager said nothing. His eyes had grown dark and fearful. His lips twitched as though he was murmuring to himself.

Hudson loosened the gun in his holster and said, "Send her out here, mister, or I'm gonna drill a bullet through your lyin' heart."

Before the manager could say anything, a girl stepped through the half-open door. She paused on the stoop beside the agent. She was a slight blonde with worn-out, worried eyes, in a shapeless gray dress faded and frayed from too many washings.

"I'm here," she said softly. "And I don't know of no Massey in these parts." She swallowed down her fear and made her voice hard. "So if you'll excuse Uncle Farley and me, we have a stage comin', and we need to get lunch on the table. Dinner don't fix itself, you know."

Several of the riders snickered. The one farthest from Hudson spit red-brown cut-plug tobacco juice onto the porch, near the agent's left foot. His name was Billy Saber, and that was what he resembled, with his long, hollow face and hooked nose under the visor of his Confederate gray cavalry hat — a saber ready to slash.

No one said anything for several seconds.

Regarding the girl, Burt Snyder spread his bewhiskered cheeks in a grin and cuffed his shapeless hat back on his head. "She's purty."

"She ain't bad," Page Hudson allowed, "but she ain't what we're here for. We're here for Massey and the two-thousand-dollar bounty on his head."

The girl frowned. "Bounty?" She glanced at her uncle.

"That's right — bounty," Dusty Dale Winget said. "Little over a year ago, he killed the son of a man named Franklin Evans, big rancher near Julesburg." A smile grew on Dusty Dale's freckled, sun-blistered face. "The son was about to carve out some whore's Adam's apple when Massey shot him. Ole Evans put a bounty on Massey's head. Started out only five hundred dollars, but no one's been able to bring the kid's head to Franklin, so he upped it."

"Massey's become right good with a gun, they say," Page Hudson said jovially.

The girl's expression turned angry. "Only because he's had to!"

"Vera!" the agent scolded her.

"Oh, what's the use of lying, Uncle Farley? These men are going to find Cuno anyway." Vera turned her beseeching gaze to the mounted men. "Please leave him alone! Please leave him and July alone! They haven't done anything to you!"

The riders exchanged glances. Dusty Dale and Burt Snyder grinned. Several horses bobbed their heads, eager to get moving. Hudson still had a look of quiet amusement on his round face with its small eyes and knobby scars.

"Sure, we'll leave 'em alone," he told the girl mildly. "Where they live?"

"We just wanna wish him and his bride a happy life," Snyder told the girl, shifting his mocking eyes to the man on his left.

"Yeah, that's it," Dusty Dale said with a hoot. "I knew he was around here. I knew we'd find that son of a bitch. Man, I'm gonna have me a gay ole time with that lucre in Denver City!"

"Please!" Vera beseeched the strangers, wringing her hands. "Can't you let them be? They're happy. They wanna start a family. . . ."

"Vera, you hold your tongue, girl," the agent admonished. He pushed her back into the cabin with one hand while regarding the riders with consternation. When he'd shut the door, he said, "Like my niece says, Cuno and July Massey are good people. They're young and they're gonna start a family. You

12

ain't got no call — bounty or not — to ride over there and stir up trouble. If Cuno killed someone, you can damn sure bet the fella had it comin'!" The agent screwed up his face. "Don't you have no conscience?"

Kenny Wilks laughed and leaned forward in his saddle, spreading his stirrups as he tensed his legs. "Mister, do we *look* like we have a conscience?"

"Well," the agent said, stubbornly crossing his arms on his chest, "I ain't tellin' you where they live. No, sir. If you find 'em, it ain't gonna be on account of me."

Their hardware gleaming in the bright sunlight, the six riders stared at the man with their hard eyes.

Finally, Hudson drew his pistol and thumbed back the hammer. "Mister," he said, "I didn't think it would."

The Remington jumped in Hudson's hands, powder smoke wafting. The station agent flew back against the cabin door, the hole in his throat leaking blood. The man clawed at his neck with both hands while he slid down the door to his butt.

Making choking sounds, he fell sideways to the porch floor and crawled feebly along the porch until Hudson shot him again, opening a hole in his back, between his shoulder blades. The agent collapsed with a grunt and lay still, his face turned toward the riders, his open eyes staring at the ants climbing in and out of the cracks between the boards.

"Damn," Hudson said, "I was aimin' that first one at his teeth."

The door clicked and opened a crack. The girl peeked through the crack, her blue eyes wide with horror. "Uncle Farley?" she said in a quaking voice, lips quivering.

Her eyes dropped, found the agent lying dead. "Oh, my God!" she cried, raising her eyes. *"You animals!"*

She withdrew her head and slammed the door.

Billy Saber turned to Hudson, showing his long teeth while stretching a grin, his long, wispy blond hair blowing beneath the forage hat. "Want me to take care of her, Page?"

"No, I sure as hell don't," Hudson growled, climbing out of his saddle. He flipped his reins to Burt Snyder and headed for the stoop. "You'd enjoy it too damn much, and we ain't here to enjoy anything but sawing Massey's head off and ridin' for Julesburg."

Hudson mounted the stoop and kicked in the door, his bull-hide chaps winging out. Stepping into the cabin's shadowy interior, he yelled, "Girl, get over here *now!*"

Dusty Dale, Clevis O'Malley, Billy Saber, Burt Snyder, and Kenny Wilks sat their mounts lazily, smiles crinkling their hard, renegade faces while they listened to the girl scream and run about the cabin knocking over furniture and throwing dishes and pans. A chair flew past the front door, which had swung halfway back to the jamb. Blond hair flying, the girl dashed past the door followed by a cursing Hudson.

The girl screamed again, shrilly. There was a loud thud, as though someone had hit the floor hard. Hudson shouted something unintelligible.

There were scuffling sounds. Hudson spoke in a low, hard voice. The girl replied, her voice brittle, the words indiscernible.

A pistol popped twice, the sharp reports echoing inside the cabin and making Clevis O'Malley jump in his saddle. "Jumpin' Jesus!" the big, dark-haired Irishman exclaimed.

A few seconds later, the door was flung open and Hudson walked through it, flushed and sweating. Jaws set angrily, he crossed the stoop, adjusted his hat, grabbed his reins back from Snyder, and mounted his buckskin.

"Come on," he snapped, reining away from the cabin and gigging the horse into a

15

gallop. "I'm tired of messin' around!"

"You find out where Massey lives?" Kenny Wilks called to him.

"What do you think?"

2

Leprechauns and elves . . .

That's what Cuno Massey half-expected to see along the wooded path upon which he and his wife strolled in the early afternoon. July Massey carried a wicker basket brimming with Juneberries.

Cuno had shot a young whitetail buck in the hills while July had been berry-picking. He'd skinned the deer and wrapped the meat in the hide, which he'd tied and carried now in a makeshift pack on his back. He carried his Winchester rifle in his right hand. He held July's free hand in his left, squeezing it lovingly.

Leprechauns and elves, maybe a fairy or two from one of the stories his mother had read to him as a child . . .

It was that kind of magical day, when the appearance of such storybook figures seemed possible, appearing and vanishing in

17

the cottonwoods shading the creek or in the berry-spotted brush running along the buttes and in the folds of the hills. Maybe a larger-than-life rabbit hip-hopping along the ferns lining that seep yonder, trailed by singing mice and fuddy-duddy porcupines.

"What are you thinking about?"

Nudged from his daydream, Cuno Massey looked at his lovely wife, whose Indian-black hair breezed about her face and long, delicate neck. July was half-Choctaw. Her eyes, the cobalt blue of a fjord-dwelling Viking, lent her an astonishing exoticness.

She usually wore men's clothes for working about the farm, but today — Sunday — she'd donned her homespun gingham dress, which snugged her girlishly round, firm bust and waist and fell in pleated folds along her legs. Her straw hat, which Cuno had bought at the mercantile in town, shaded her forehead and eyes and caused her to tip her head back to regard him from under the broad brim. It gave her a sweet, girlish appearance. The black ribbon around the bullet crown fluttered in the breeze.

Cuno shrugged. "Nothin' much."

"Come on," July urged, tugging on his hand, "tell me."

"Why?"

"'Cause if you don't I'm gonna start

thinkin' you're settin' your hat for another girl." She gave him a mock-jealous look, but her eyes were bright with humor.

Self-conscious, he scowled and shrugged again, kicked at a stone in the trail. "I was thinkin' about elves and leprechauns." His rawboned face flushed a deeper red under his ruddy tan. "And fairies . . ."

July laughed with mocking delight. "And fairies?"

Cuno Massey stopped and, as though defending his flight of fancy, said, "Look at that meadow over yonder, beyond the creek. Look at the water flowing over the rocks. Heck, look at all this, July. What a fine day!"

July released his hand to drag wisps of blowing hair from her eyes as she studied the scene, smiling brightly. She turned the smile on her young husband, who resembled a Viking in his own right.

Under the brim of his wide, tan hat, Cuno's face was broad and handsome. It appeared chiseled from smooth stone, the eyes wide and deep, the nose a straight, broad line. His hard, dimpled chin gave him an air of stalwart resolution. He stood five feet ten inches, and he carried the bulk of his 190 pounds in his shoulders and arms, straining his chambray shirt and the bone buttons across his slabbed chest. His blue denims stretched taut over his work-sculpted thighs. On his feet he wore scuffed, high-topped boots into which his pants were stuffed.

"Cuno Massey, you're right," July told him through a cheerful smile. "I never knew you to be so chatty, but I sure am glad to see you happy for a change."

"It's nice to be feelin' happy," Cuno said, staring into the sun-dappled meadow. "It's nice to finally stop feeling like a hunted animal. It's nice to feel like a normal fella with a farm and a wife" — he lowered his eyes to her still-flat belly — "and a family on the way."

"Do you think it's finally over?"

She was referring to the men who had been gunning for Cuno since he'd hunted down and killed the two men who had murdered his father and stepmother. Rolf Anderson and Sammy Spoon had been known for their prowess with guns. By killing them and several other men he'd had to gun down during his search for his family's killers, Cuno had earned an unwanted reputation as a shootist — a reputation that more than one tinhorn had tried to surpass.

Then there was also his killing of Vince Evans and the bounty Evans's father had placed on Cuno's head.

Cuno shrugged and adjusted the rifle in

his hand, the hide-wrapped venison pack on his back. "It's hard to say, but it's been five months since I've been challenged."

"It helps that our neighbors play dumb about us, but I think the trigger-itchy tinhorns and the bounty hunters have done forgot about you. At least, that's what I hope with all my heart."

Cuno nodded. "Either that, or they don't think it's worth riding this far off the beaten path for a lead swap."

"I don't care what the reason is," July said. "I just hope it's true. If anything happened to you, Cuno Massey, I'd" — she shook her head and frowned with deep frustration — "I'd hunt the varmints down and tear their hearts out with my fingernails!"

Cuno laughed and put an arm around his seventeen-year-old bride. Cuno himself was only nineteen, but the ordeal with his father's killers had aged him. Sometimes he felt downright old. "Easy there, Wes Hardin. Nothin's gonna happen to me — at least, not till after I've raised a whole passel of our young'uns and seen another passel of grandkids grown."

"It better not." July set her basket down, wrapped her arms around his neck, and kissed him passionately, moving her hands across his broad shoulders, loving the safe

21

feeling his hard body always gave her.

When she pulled away, he winked and smiled at her lustily. "It's hotter'n blazes out here. Let's go for a wade."

"I can do you one better than that," July said, mirroring his lusty grin. She led Cuno to the edge of the water and set her basket down beside a rock. "Let's go for a swim."

Sitting on a rock, she pulled off her shoes and socks, then stood and began unbuttoning her dress. Cuno had been her first lover, but he had never known another girl more earthy and frank. The former Miss July Summer did much more than satisfy her husband's manly cravings under the bedcovers. She fueled them, until he often thought he was going to die of lust before the next sundown.

In a moment, she stood proudly naked before him, her pert, pink-nippled breasts jutting, her coarse, dark hair framing them beautifully. Her legs were long and shapely, her hips and bottom round and tight. A more lovely, enticing visage he had never seen.

"Last one in's a rotten egg!" Laughing, she ran splashing into the creek, the water glistening like diamonds around her almond thighs.

Halfway across the stream, she dove shallowly and came up glistening, wiping water from her eyes with her hands, blowing it from her lips. It took Cuno only a minute to pry off his boots, shed his clothes, and join her, swimming out and engulfing her in his arms with a joyful whoop. She returned his kiss, wrapping her arms around his thick, sunburned neck, her legs clinging to his back.

At length, she pulled her head away from his and dropped her right hand into the water between his legs. "You'd make a good boat, honey," she said with a giggle.

"How's that?" he asked, grunting with pleasure.

"You have one heck of a rudder!"

He feigned shock. But he'd actually gotten quite accustomed to her earthy humor since meeting her nearly a year ago while heading north on the Bozeman Trail. "Mrs. Massey, proper girls do not give voice to such a sentiment."

"Oh, shut up and make love to me, my handsome, big-ruddered husband!" she beseeched, and closed her mouth over his once more.

They made love in the water, and again in a soft patch of grass along the stream. They dozed in the golden sunlight filtering through the leaves, entwined in each other's arms and legs — a delicate, black-haired beauty clinging to the muscular Viking lad whose hard, thick body fairly swallowed her up.

Finally, they dressed, chatting quietly and dreamily about the future. They discussed the new ground Cuno would break next year, the irrigation ditch he would dig from the river, adding several acres of wheat to their tilled acreage. They planned the addition to the cabin he intended to build with the help of Farley Grissom, who ran the stage station on the other side of the Burnt Creek Hills and who had taken the young couple under his wing. Farley had helped Cuno build his and July's cabin and barn and dig post holes for the corral, while Grissom's niece, Vera, had become good friends with July. It was important to have friends out here, in this rugged, isolated land, so far off the beaten path.

Seclusion reduced trouble from outsiders, but it could get damn lonely out here. . . .

As Cuno and July headed down the trail to their cabin, curved around the lightning-split cottonwood, and entered the farmyard, Cuno froze, squeezing July's hand suddenly, protectively. As he looked around, concerned lines etched his forehead. He released July's hand and turned his gaze to the corral, where a horse and two mules stood unmoving in a rear corner, a dubious cast to their stares.

"What's the matter?"

"I don't know." He had a sudden bad sense of things, and the feeling was growing.

He looked at the single-story cabin nestled in the bushes on the north side of the yard. Seeing nothing unusual, he shuttled his gaze to the log barn, which he hadn't gotten around to chinking yet. The single door hung open. Had he left it that way?

Again, he turned to the corral. His paint skewbald, Renegade, trotted away from the mules, stopped, and rippled its withers. His dark eyes rolled toward the cabin, and his ears twitched.

Cuno turned to the cabin, studied the closed door and quiet stoop. Tree shadows canted across the earthen roof as the light of the west-angling sun turned golden. Sudden movement behind the cabin caught Cuno's eye.

There it was again. Back in the cotton-woods, behind the tin-roofed privy, a horse swished its tail.

"July," Cuno rasped through gritted teeth as he dropped the deerskin bundle from his shoulder and began raising his rifle, "head for the barn!"

She looked around, hesitant, confused. "Why . . . what?"

"Go!"

A rifle cracked. A bullet spanged off a rock six inches from Cuno's right boot. The shot had come from the barn. Cuno heaved July toward the hay crib before the corral, yelling, "Take cover!"

Two more shots exploded as, wheeling, Cuno brought his rifle up and jacked a shell in the chamber. A man stood in the open loft door, his own rifle aimed at Cuno, who dove to his right just as the gunman's rifle cracked. Cuno rolled off his shoulder and came to his haunches, again raising the rifle. He fired and cocked several times, the spent shells arcing over his shoulder.

The ambusher tumbled forward out of the loft, somersaulting on his way to the ground and landing with a thud and whush of blown dust.

Cuno yelled for July.

The only reply was more gunfire and the whistle of slugs around his head.

Firing into the coulee behind the barn while dodging bullets fired from various spots around the cabin, Cuno ducked behind a rock pile and jerked his wild eyes toward the hay crib.

All he saw were July's straw hat and the

wicker basket lying amidst the scattered berries.

"July!"

Again, the only reply was the gunfire, bullets chinging off the stones and spraying him with shards of lead and rock. A bullet split the air over his left shoulder. The shot had come from behind him. He fired two rounds into the coulee, crouched to reload the Winchester from his cartridge belt, then turned toward the cabin.

Smoke puffed in the open doorway, obscuring the figure of a medium-tall man with close-set eyes and a funnel-brimmed hat with hammered silver disks decorating the crown. A bullet seared a furrow along Cuno's left cheekbone as more smoke puffed in the broken kitchen window, right of the door.

Resting his right shoulder against the rocks, Cuno opened fire on the figure standing in the cabin's doorway, triggering four quick rounds, then firing two more rounds at the window. With a pained yell, the gunman jerked back from the window as wood sprayed from the frame.

Another gunman fired from a corner of the cabin, the bullet sizzling off Cuno's ear as he dove forward, triggering his Winchester. The man gave a surprised jerk and bolted back behind the wall. As he did,

Cuno caught a glimpse of a Confederate cavalry hat and stringy blond hair.

"Clevis, where the hell are you, man?" someone yelled from inside the cabin.

"Both my guns are jammed, Page!" replied a baritone from a knoll about thirty yards east of the cabin.

"Goddamnit, you stupid sons o' bitches," yelled the man in the cabin. "If you can't bring down one man without getting yourselves all shot to hell, then for chrissakes pull out!"

"Pull out?" an incredulous voice replied.

"Pull out!" returned the man in the cabin. "We'll come back for him later!"

There was one more shot from the corner of the cabin, and Cuno caught another glimpse of the gray hat before it retreated behind the wall. The gunmen around the cabin ceased firing, and Cuno could hear muffled voices growing small as the men retreated.

The man in the coulee, however, was still triggering rounds. Cursing and snarling like a cornered wolverine, Cuno gained his feet and ran out from behind the rock pile. He sprinted across the green, knee-high wheat toward the cut flanking the barn.

Smoke puffed ahead, and the gunman's rifle barked. Cuno weaved as the bullet buzzed and whistled around him, then plunked into the ground near his feet.

"You son of a bitch!" he yelled, drawing near the coulee, stopping, and raising the Winchester.

The gunman's hatted head appeared at the lip of the coulee's ridge. It disappeared as Cuno pulled the trigger, blowing up a gout of sod where the head had been only a half moment before. Seconds later, the man reappeared, running away toward the creek curving through burr oaks and cottonwoods behind the coulee.

Cuno jacked another shell and bolted into a run. He jumped into the coulee, nearly losing his balance as his left foot clipped a gopher hole, and resumed running full-out toward the retreating rifleman, pumping hard toward the creek flashing silver through the trees.

His heart raced and his jaws were clamped tight with mute fury. He ran hard, chewing up ground, gaining on the rifleman entering the trees.

"Stop and face me, you yellow son of a bitch!"

The man stopped, chest heaving, and wheeled, bringing his rifle around. Cuno didn't give the man a chance to raise the carbine. He snugged the Winchester against his shoulder and fired.

29

The gunman flew back, arms flailing for balance, dropping the rifle and tumbling into the creek with a scream and a splash.

Cuno ran to the stream, made sure the man was dead — a skinny redhead with large freckles and a bullet through his chest. Then he turned and ran to the cabin. The cry of retreat could have been a ruse.

Mounting the cabin's two steps, he bounded across the porch and threw the door wide. The cabin, with its hodgepodge of rough-hewn furniture, woven rugs, and hanging pots, was empty. A splash of blood marked the board floor between the window and the table littered with shattered glass.

Looking around the single room again, Cuno saw that the rear door off the kitchen was partly open. He ran to it, looked around, his rifle held ready, then ran out behind the privy.

The horses were gone, leaving only prints where the ambushers had arrived from the east. All six horses had fled west in a hurry, though two of them had to be riderless.

Wheeling, breathing hard, sweat basting his shirt to his chest and back, Cuno ran back around the house and across the yard, yelling for July.

When he'd last seen her, she'd been bolting toward the hay crib.

Hoping to find her hiding safely there now, he ducked through the corral and froze.

"July!"

He staggered toward her, his face bleached, his eyes bulging with horror. July lay on her side on the hard-packed ground behind the crib, her hair forming a black fan beneath her head. Blood soaked the bosom of her dress.

Cuno froze, shuddered, his boots glued to the ground where he stood staring. For a long time, he was unable to understand what he was seeing, as though lost in a dream in which none of the images fit together logically.

Finally, he stumbled forward. "July . . . oh, God . . . July . . ." He knelt down and took her gently in his arms. Her body was limp but still warm.

"July, please," he rasped, his eyes wild with shock and disbelief. "July . . . no . . . please," he begged her, over and over again, until he was crouched over her, hugging her lifeless body, pressing his cheek to hers. Tears streamed down his face. His body jerked with sobs.

"July!" he cried. "July! Oh, God, please . . . don't be dead!"

The blood on her breast formed a wide crimson bib. There was more on her back,

31

where the bullet had exited after tearing through her heart. Her Nordic-blue eyes stared up at him through half-shut lids, unseeing.

His own heart threatened to burst through his chest as he held her tightly in his big arms, rocking her as though to gently nudge her life back into her, refusing to believe his beloved could really be gone.

"Ju-*lyyyy!*"

3

"Goddamnit, Page, I need a rest!" Kenny Wilks complained, crouched over his wounded left arm.

He'd been straggling back in the four-man procession. Now he rode up past O'Malley and Billy Saber to Hudson, who had stopped to scan their back trail.

The sun was angling low, stretching shadows out from a cluster of burr oaks and a nearby sandstone shelf.

"How bad you hit?" Hudson asked.

"Look at me bleed! You never said he raised hob with a rifle."

Wilks was the youngest of the surviving gunmen. He was a comical figure, slight of stature beneath a baggy town suit complete with bowler hat and gold watch chain. Only, instead of a dress shirt beneath the broadcloth jacket, he wore a smoke-stained buckskin shirt. Instead of brogans, he wore Texas-built boots, old and worn to a floury white.

As ridiculous as he looked, Wilks was rock-cold efficient when it came to close-range shooting with a handgun. He'd been honing his cold-steel talent since the day when he was only thirteen and he'd shot his schoolmaster in southern Arkansas and lit out to make a name for himself as a frontier gunslick.

"I told you he killed Rolf Anderson and Sammy Spoon, ye damn tinhorn." Hudson leaned over to inspect Wilks's bloody arm. "It's just a graze, Kenny. You'll live."

"Graze or not, I can't ride no more today. This arm needs cleanin', an' I need some whiskey for the pain."

Clevis O'Malley was thumbing cartridges from his belt into his open pistol cylinder. "I say we ditch this stupid son of a bitch, Page, and go back. My guns *were* jammed. They ain't jammed now."

Hudson's small, cold eyes stared at the prairie hogbacks rolling off to the horizon. Lightning flashed in a china-white, anvil-shaped thunderhead no more than ten miles away. "That goddamn Burt's the one who started the shootin', missed Massey with that wild shot o' his." Hudson spit angrily. "Good riddance to that knot-headed blowfly."

"Let's go back and finish what we started," the burly, dark-bearded O'Malley urged. Seeds and dust flecked his beard and bushy brows. He closed his Colt's loading gate, spun the gun by a finger, and holstered it — all in one slick motion. O'Malley might have been big, but he did not lack grace.

Hudson fingered his chin, his eyes thoughtful. "He'd be ready for us now. He's good. That son of a bitch's good, for a kid." Hudson shook his head quickly. "Besides, that thunder-boomer's building right mean-like. It'll be rainin' and hailin' in an hour."

Billy Saber grinned and gave a whoop. "Man, I bet that kid's sore. Did you see his girl crawl back behind the hay crib?"

Hudson glanced at him. "Yeah, who shot her?"

"Well, hell, it was you, Page!" Billy said. "It was one o' those first coupla shots you meant for the kid."

Hudson was incredulous. "Me?"

"I'm certain sure! It wasn't me. Hell, I didn't wanna hit her. She carved a nice little figure — that half-breed did. She woulda been all kinds o' won'erful fun tonight under the army wool."

"You sure it wasn't Clevis?"

"I didn't shoot no girl — half-breed or not," O'Malley countered, indignant. "I was

35

extra careful. We coulda sold her to the Co-manches on our way to Mexico."

"Well, goddamnit!" Hudson said, palming his six-shooter, hefting it in his hand. "This is a new gun; it's weighted different than my old one. I guess I haven't practiced enough yet. Sure am sorry, boys. I felt like stickin' that little filly with my own pickle tonight."

"That's okay, Page," Billy Saber said, slapping Hudson's right shoulder consolingly. "There's plenty women around. We get desperate enough, we can find us a stagecoach, maybe find some little darlin' in a soft silk dress."

Kenny Wilks sucked air through his crooked teeth, which he still bared in pain as he crouched over his saddle horn. His left sleeve was soaked with blood. "I hate to interrupt all the friendly palaver, but do you boys mind if we find somewhere I can get this arm doctored . . . *before I bleed to goddamn death?*"

Page Hudson gave the wounded rider a look of mock injury. "We're goin', Kenny . . . we're goin'." He turned his horse around to the southwest. "But try to keep your friggin' pants on, will you? Only little girls and Nancy-boys scream."

· It was dark as night and raining hard when the four riders halted their horses on a butte over a long, low shack, a small barn, and two corrals. The cabin's windows were lit and Hudson could make out, by a pinprick of umber light, someone smoking on the porch.

"Lord's Roadhouse," Hudson yelled above the pattering rain. "You'll find some whiskey here, Kenny. Maybe even a girl or two."

Hudson gigged his horse down the muddy butte, the buckskin sliding in the runneling water and slippery grass. The others followed him into the yard. Lightning flashed and thunder peeled, causing the mounts to crow-hop, splashing in the puddles.

"Name yourselves!" a man called from the porch.

Hudson recognized the voice. "Who you expectin', Bella? Federal marshals?" Hudson chuckled as he climbed down from his saddle, rain sluicing from his hat brim.

"Can't be too careful," the man on the porch said, his hand still on his pistol butt.

He was a tall, portly gent, his gray hair pulled back in a ponytail beneath a broad, high-crowned Stetson. He wore a yellow slicker, one side tucked behind the six-shooter and holster thonged low on his right thigh. A short quirley glowed brightly in his free hand.

Hudson tossed his reins up to Clevis

O'Malley and mounted the porch. "Stayin' outta trouble, Bella?"

"Can't say as much fer you, I see," Lord said as he watched Kenny Wilks crawl painfully down from his saddle, crooking his injured arm close to his chest.

"Ah, he's just scratched," Hudson said. "How's the whiskey?"

"Nectar of the gods, Page," Lord said, his teeth painting a pale grin in the darkness. "Nectar of the gods."

"That bad, eh?" Hudson said with a grimace. "Well, beggars can't be choosers." Turning to O'Malley, he said, "Clevis, be a good boy and bed our horses down in the barn, will you?"

O'Malley glowered down from atop his dun, holding Hudson's reins like a turd. "It's Billy's turn to—"

Hudson shook his head. "It's Kenny's turn, but he ain't able, so you do it and don't give me any shit." He looked hard at O'Malley, who returned the gaze.

O'Malley blinked slowly, finally shrugged. You didn't push Hudson too hard. O'Malley had found that out when Hudson had taken over as leader several months ago, leaving the man who'd challenged him with a knife poking out of his Adam's apple.

With a mocking whoop, Saber tossed the

big Irishman his reins.

"Hey, don't forget Kenny's!" Saber said, grabbing Wilks's reins off the hitching post and tossing those too to O'Malley, who accepted them stiffly, his broad nose curled with a sneer.

Hudson shook his head as though at foolish children, and opened the roadhouse door. Slowly, he stepped inside and swept his gaze across the lamplit room before him, one hand on his gun butt. He'd been joking about lawmen, but you never knew. He had to figure bounty hunters were after him as well.

Several men sat about the low, rectangular room cluttered with plank tables and benches and smoke-belching lamps hanging from joists. The smell of wet wool, leather, pine smoke, and a meaty stew wafted over him. Two men nearest Hudson regarded him cautiously, hands on their holstered guns.

"It's all right, boys," Hudson said coolly. "As long as there ain't any badge-toters in here."

There was a short pause interrupted by only a ticking stove in which burning wood shifted. Someone said from a cot behind a timber post, "Hey, Page, you know lawmen stay clear of Bella's — less'n they're lookin' to get turned toe-down, that is."

A girl squealed at this. She was lying beside and half under the man who'd made the joke, on the right side of the room. A buffalo skin partition had been thrown back, revealing them. Neither had qualms about frolicking in public.

"I reckon," Hudson said as he moved into the room, swinging his head from left to right. Cautiously, he checked out the faces of the five other men in the place, all of whom he recognized from the outlaw trail. Some he liked, some he disliked but not enough for a lead swap — at least, not as far as he was concerned. Just in case his sentiment was not shared by all, he kept his hand close to his pistol. "But like Bella says, you can't be too careful."

Hudson stopped before the man on the cot. "How you doin', Chet?"

Chet Dupree grabbed the naked knee of the girl beside him. "How's it look?"

Hudson appraised the girl — a fleshy blonde wrapped in only a blanket, paint smeared on her cheeks and around her eyes giving her a clownish look. She was a whore from somewhere; Hudson couldn't remember where. He was sure he'd had her at one time or another.

"I see you're doin' all right."

The girl giggled as Dupree nuzzled her

40

neck. Chet's eyes rose to Kenny Wilks, hurrying down the middle of the room toward the kitchen at the rear. Blood oozed between fingers clamped over the wound. "Kenny's lookin' a little worse for the wear."

"He'll be all right," Hudson said, heading for the plank bar, behind which Bella Lord had taken a soldierly position, fists on the planks, waiting for orders.

Hudson passed a man dressed in high-toned gambler's garb playing poker with a man Hudson recognized as the safecracker Clem Talbert. Hudson raked his eyes over both men, who raked their own eyes over him blandly, defensive as dogs, then swung his gaze toward the bar.

As he did so, he caught a glimpse of someone lying on a cot behind a tattered deer-hide curtain. Long hair, light brown skin, womanly curves.

Frowning with interest, Hudson wheeled from the bar and swept the hide curtain back on its rope. The girl on the cot padded with several buffalo hides gave a start, and quickly covered a naked thigh with an army blanket, dropping the yellow-covered book she'd been reading.

She was a slight, slender Mexican with chestnut hair falling down her back to the jeans she'd bunched for a pillow. A small, purple birthmark shone on her neck, just below her left ear. She was short and willowy, with almond skin and dark brown eyes. Large, full breasts strained the cotton chemise hanging loosely from her shoulders, the prominent nipples silhouetted by the dim lamp behind her.

"Hey, there," someone said behind Hudson.

Page had barely heard. He stared hard at the girl, puzzlement and surprise etched on his thin brows, the light of recognition growing in his eyes. "Well, I'll be gee-goddamned. *Marcella?*"

She glared at him, as angry as she was afraid. Her full upper lip curled in a sneer easily, as if it had been made for such an expression. "Get away from me!"

"Hey, there," said the voice again behind Hudson. It was closer this time, louder. Boots squawked a floorboard. Hudson turned to see the gambler standing only a few feet away, his cards in his right hand, which boasted an amethyst pinkie ring. The other hand was on the pearl-handled Colt in his oily black holster. A frown wrinkled his auburn mustache.

"What do you think you're doing there?" he asked.

"Whatever the hell I want," Hudson said.

"Beat it, pasteboard boy."

"That's my girl."

"She's an old friend, and we got business. Now git, sonny."

"Wade, please," the girl said in a heavy Spanish accent, holding the blanket over her breasts. "He shot my fiancé!"

Hudson turned to her, throwing his head back with a laugh. "Fianc-what? You were Rick's whore, you purty little bean-eater! Now, tell this sharpie to back off. We got business, you and me."

"Listen, mister," the gambler said, pinching Hudson's left shoulder.

Hudson jerked his gaze toward the man, lowered his eyes to the hand on his shoulder. He didn't say anything. Neither did the gambler. Hudson lifted his eyes again to the gambler's hard face, the outlaw's flat eyes kindling with anger.

The man must have read Hudson's intentions, because he quickly released Hudson's shoulder, dropping his hand to his pistol. He'd read the intention too late. He'd barely gotten the butt of the pistol out of the holster when Page had flicked his own revolver out, jabbed it into the gambler's gut, and fired twice.

The room rocked with the muffled barks. Smoke wafted. The Mexican girl screamed.

The gambler grunted loudly, stumbled backward into the table upon which he'd been playing cards, knocking it over. His opponent stood quickly, knocking back his own chair, cards in his hand.

"Hey, hey, hey!" the gambler's opponent yelled with surprise, watching the gambler fall over the edge of the overturned table, clutching his guts and moving his legs, as though trying to bull the table across the room. He and the table moved only a foot or two.

The gambler cursed, sighed, and expired.

Hudson turned his smoking gun on the rest of the room.

4

"Anyone else want some of this?" Hudson asked the others. He didn't dare turn his back until he knew what the response to the gambler's death would be.

None of the other men said anything.

Clevis O'Malley and Billy Saber were standing by the door. They'd been wrestling out of their wet slickers when the ruckus with the girl and the gambler started. They stood now regarding the other men in the room, hands on their holstered gun butts in case Hudson needed backing.

It didn't look like he did. The responses stretched the gamut between furled brows and glassy-eyed grins. But no one seemed inclined to avenge the gambler's death. A pump handle squawked in the back kitchen where Kenny Wilks was doctoring his arm.

The gambler's opponent still stood over the overturned table, his cards in his hand.

"Shit," he said, happily surprised. "That sumbitch damn near cleaned me out!" He guffawed, threw down his cards, and crouched over the table, collecting his losings. "Thanks!"

The other men didn't appear to be a threat, but the girl was another matter.

Hudson was turning toward her when she cried, "You son of a bitch!" She planted a hard right cross on his jaw, snapping his head back and sending painful flares behind his eyes. She was coming at him again, her hair and fists flying, when, regaining his senses, he ducked under her blows, picked her up in his arms, and threw her like a sack of corn onto her cot.

She screamed a curse before her head connected with the cot frame. Then she lay moaning and holding her head in her arms, kicking her bare legs.

"Excuse us, boys," Hudson drew the deerhide partition closed.

He turned to the girl, who was cursing softly, her dark hair obscuring her face, her head in her arms. "Hello, Marcella."

Her eyes found him and froze, and her face paled with horrified recognition.

"I looked high and low for you," Hudson said. "For a whole damn year. I give up on ye, thought ye was dead." He chuckled softly

46

and moved to the cot, stood stiffly over her. His face was flushed — all but the two matching scars, which were white as new ice against the red. "Where is it?"

When she did not answer, he said again, "Where?"

She lowered her arms. Her face too was flushed with anger, her eyes large and slick with tears. "Where is what?"

"The silver crucifix. The one that belonged to your mother."

She studied him silently, her dark eyes dubious. "I do not know what you are talking about."

"Sure you do." Hudson smacked her hard with his gloved hand.

Her head whipped back, hair flying again. She lay stunned, breathing heavily. When she regained her senses, she turned her face to him, her features pinched with rage. *"Bastard!"*

"Where is it?"

"Why do you want my mother's crucifix?" she yelled, voice brittle with anger and exasperation.

Hudson crawled onto the cot and grabbed Marcella's chin in his right hand, staring into her eyes. "Just tell me where it is, you stupid whore!"

Knowing he'd find it sooner or later anyway, and having no idea why he wanted it, she said in a hard, low voice, "In my bag!"

"Where?"

She pointed toward the wall, where a worn carpetbag lay on its side, clothes spilling onto the floor. Hudson picked it up, rummaged around, until he froze with his hand deep inside the bag.

He smiled at Marcella sitting on the bed, strands of sweat-damp hair pasted to her cheeks. Her hate-filled eyes were curious and skeptical, wondering what in the name of the saints this crazy man was up to. She'd kept her dead mother's crucifix close to her since leaving the Mexican village in which she'd been raised. To her it was an heirloom, but she doubted it was worth very much money. If it had been, she'd have hawked it herself.

She couldn't imagine why Hudson wanted it.

Slowly, Hudson pulled his hand out of the bag. In his closed fist was the crucifix — eight inches long by four inches wide by one inch deep. Hudson gazed at the crucifix, smiled lustily, swallowed. With his other hand, he tripped the cross's tiny latch and flipped it open.

He looked into the cross-shaped box lined with red velvet. A piece of yellowed paper lay folded within.

"I'll be goddamned," he whispered.

He set the open crucifix on the windowsill, quickly removed his gloves, then removed the paper from the crucifix and carefully unfolded it, regarding it with keen interest, beads of sweat glistening on his sandy brow.

On the bed, Marcella watched wide-eyed. She'd carried the crucifix with her nearly everywhere in her bag — it was too large and bulky to wear around her neck — but she hadn't looked inside it for years. Her mother had stored only pins and needles in it.

As Hudson studied the paper, tilting it toward the lamp, his lascivious smile widened. His eyes bulged.

"What is it?" Marcella whispered, wiping a tear from her cheek with the back of her right hand. "What's in my crucifix?"

Hudson slid his eyes to her. "Rick's map to the gold we stole and he tried to run off with — dirty, cheatin' bastard." He kept his taunting voice low so the others would not hear. "Right here." He shook the paper slightly. "You been carrying it around for over a year, in your momma's old cross."

Marcella's mind raced. The room spun around her.

"What are you saying?" she whispered.

The outlaw chuckled. Bending low, he

thrust his mocking face toward hers, waving the map high in one hand. "The map to twenty-five thousand dollars in gold bars we stole off that stage. You been carrying it around all these months. Just before I killed Rick, I got him to tell me where he'd hid it. He said you had the map, in your momma's crucifix." He poked her chest with his finger. "But you didn't know it."

Marcella stared at him, flabbergasted. She raised her hands to her head, smoothing her hair back from her temples as though trying to keep her skull from exploding. "I thought you were chasing me to kill me." She said it softly, wonderingly, as though to herself.

"I wouldn't kill you, Marci-baby. I mean, sure, you and my brother were tryin' to hornswoggle me, take all the gold for yourselves." He planted a hand on her naked thigh, squeezing. "But you're too good-lookin' to kill. . . . "

She kicked her foot out and slapped his hand away from her thigh. "Get away from me, you pig!"

"Now, that's no way to talk, Marci. Hell, we were nearly family, you and me. If you show me a real good time tonight, maybe I'll shave you off a few dollars worth of dust."

She still stared at Hudson blindly, distraught over the fact that she'd been unwittingly carrying around the map to the gold Rick had buried, the gold she herself had yearned for and dreamed about ever since Hudson had killed Rick fourteen months ago. It was no surprise that Rick hadn't told her about the map. She hadn't trusted him any more than he had trusted her.

Why had she never opened the crucifix?

"Get away from me," she told Hudson again, her voice brittle now, not so much with anger as defeat.

"Ah, come on, Marci," Hudson said as he shoved the map down into his boot, then pulled his jeans over the top. "Would it be so bad, showin' ole Page a good time?"

He climbed slowly onto the cot, smiling at her, his eyes pinned to her breasts.

"I said get away from me!" she screamed, lashing out with her legs. She wouldn't sleep with Page Hudson for all the gold in the world. "Get *awayyyy!*"

Hudson grabbed her legs and crawled on top of her, holding her head down with a handful of hair. "Shut up, you goddamn whore!" he raged, no longer worrying about who heard what.

She screamed again. He cut the scream off with a sharp blow to her chin, and she fell limp beneath him, her eyes fluttering closed, her head turning to the side and canting downward.

"Ah, don't go to sleep on me . . . Marci, you whore," Hudson lamented. He shook her shoulders. "Come on, Marci . . . wake up, damn ye. Celebrate with me, bitch."

The girl only sighed. Her eyelids fluttered again and lay still. Hudson offered a sigh of his own. "Ah, shit." He crawled off the bed and gained his feet. "Oh, well, I'm too tired anyhow."

Feeling the map inside his right boot, he formed a fresh smile. He might not be getting a piece of the best-looking filly in the territory tonight, but he was rich, by God.

Rich.

With a flourish, he threw the deer-hide curtain back and stepped into the main room, where Bella Lord was feeding pine logs to the wood stove adjacent to the makeshift bar. Someone had dragged the gambler outside and righted the table where he'd been gambling. Clevis O'Malley and Billy Saber sat there now, playing two-handed poker for matchsticks.

"Everything all right, Page?" O'Malley asked, chewing a matchstick.

"Clevis, my man," Hudson said, planting a hand on the big man's shoulder and giving a gentle squeeze, "everything's just peachy."

He turned to Lord. "Bella," he said buoyantly as he walked over and slapped both hands on the bar planks, "drinks all around!"

On the cot, only fifteen feet from where Page Hudson and his two compatriots played cards and drank whiskey, Marcella Jiminez regained her senses. The fog lifted slowly, her head thudding dully, her jaw feeling as though someone had hammered a spike through the joint.

She looked around the half-closed curtain, saw Hudson at the nearby table, and closed her eyes again, feigning sleep. She remembered the crucifix. She'd been carrying a map to Rick's gold cache all these months, and all the while she'd been scraping the barrel's raw bottom to make ends meet. . . .

And now here she was, still penniless, the gambler she'd taken up with two weeks ago in Alamosa dead, the map to the stolen gold stashed in Page Hudson's boot.

Madre Maria . . .

While she lay there silently fuming, she found herself wishing she'd never even known about the map even as she pondered a way of getting it back.

Maybe she shouldn't have been so hasty earlier when Hudson had wanted to "celebrate." He would be drinking heavily. Maybe, if she could lure him back and wait until he'd passed out, she could stick a knife in his heart and confiscate the map.

She thought it over, fighting her own reluctance, quelling the bile welling in her gut when she thought of that disgusting, fish-eyed gringo between her legs. Finally, conjuring images of the gold — twenty-five thousand dollars — she felt her reluctance ease, a calmness tempered by an edgy anticipation washing over her.

"Oh," she said, not too loudly but loudly enough to be heard at the table, "where am I . . . what . . . ?"

She let her voice trail off alluringly. It worked; Hudson had heard. She heard him snicker.

"Boys," he said, the legs of his chair squawking back across the warped wood floor, "I'm out."

"Oh, no, Page," Billy Saber said, snickering and winking one eye. "I think you're in."

When Hudson had had his fill of Marcella an hour later, he curled up behind her, curling his legs into hers, wrapping his wiry arms around her neck and cupping her breasts in his hands.

"Now, if you're thinkin' you're gonna get

my little map back after I'm asleep, let me warn you, Marci, my Mescin rose," he said, blowing his fetid whiskey breath in her face, "I'm a very, very light sleeper."

With that, he pecked her cheek, gave her breasts a final squeeze, and with a self-satisfied sigh, reclined his head sideways on the pillow.

Turned away from him, Marcella Jiminez stiffened. She pressed her eyes closed and muttered a curse.

5

Cuno Massey felt like a lifeless husk, a stone statue, as he stabbed his spade into the firm ground and kicked the blade down with his boot. He tore a sod chunk loose and flipped it aside, then kicked the spade into the ground once more.

As he worked, his mind dulled so that he was only dimly aware of his surroundings and of what he was doing. It was like an inner safety catch, to keep him from returning to the appalling, inconceivable fact that his wife of barely a year had been taken.

He tossed away another chunk of sod and dirt and turned back to the rectangular form he'd cut with his spade on the hillside overlooking his cabin. He repeated the maneuver until he'd left only a rectangle of dark-brown dirt webbed with grass roots and occasional stones and chips of old bison bones.

Then he began digging deeper.

As he did so, he did not look at the long, blanket-wrapped bundle lying several feet away. To do so, he knew in some faraway cavern of his consciousness, would buckle his knees and fill him with such grief that his grisly task would be impossible.

He kept his eyes on the hole, on the dirt and stones he kicked loose and heaved onto the pile of torn sod. He wore his Colt on his right hip. His gaze was rock-hard sober. His face was bleached white, mottled red around his neck. The sun was nearly down and the air was cooling, but he sweated through his shirt as he worked.

He wasn't aware of the sensation of sweating, however. He wasn't aware of anything except for an inner scream muffled to a raking whisper as though originating from a long way off.

After an hour had passed, he was several feet down in the earth. He'd removed his hat and shirt and wore only his neckerchief. He had not rested or even paused in his labor.

His wide, round shoulders and corded arms bulged, the ironlike sinews of his flat belly expanding and contracting as he pivoted and raised the shovel, releasing its load. His blond hair lay sweat-curled to his head and neck, dripping moisture onto his shoulders. The blood on his bullet-burned right cheek had dried to jelly.

Finally, when the hole was as deep as he was tall — nearly six feet — he tossed the shovel out and heaved himself out after it. He stood above the hole, gazing down. It was too dark to see the bottom of the hole, but he stared at it anyway, for a long time, unable to turn to the blanket-wrapped bundle beside him.

Consigning his young wife to a cold grave was inconceivable.

Finally, forcing himself, feeling grief fill him once more, squeezing his heart, he turned to the blanket. July could not possibly be within those folds, just lying there, saying nothing, making no movement whatever.

But she was.

The reaffirmed knowledge made him gasp audibly, his chest jerking upward as his lungs filled with the cool, damp air. He knelt beside the bundle. Unable to ward off the sobs, he gave into them once more as he took her into his arms and held her, and cried for a long time.

He wasn't sure how much time had passed before he was standing over the carefully rounded grave, staring down at the head-board he'd erected, his hat held before him in both hands. Numbly, he recited a prayer, but broke it off before he was done, squeezing his eyes closed against a fresh onslaught of tears, and saying merely, "Good-bye, July. I'll miss you forever."

Sniffing back his tears, he donned his hat, picked up his shirt, and ran it over his face. Slowly, staring at the grave, unable to let her go, he donned the shirt, buttoned it, then pulled the blade out of the sod.

He regarded the grave once more, then forced himself to turn and start back down the hill. His knees were weak and his feet were heavy, as though he were walking through quicksand.

A sickle, summer-bright moon rode high in the sky, illuminating several cloud wisps dimming the stars.

Cuno paused at the bottom of the hill. The dark farmyard, trimmed in milky moonlight, appeared abandoned. He listened, hearing only the breeze in the brush and frogs croaking down by the seep.

The killers had said they'd return for Cuno later. In the back of his mind, he'd been hoping, waiting for them.

But so far, they had not come. That meant he would have to go after them.

If he knew one thing in his grief-ravaged mind, it was that the killers would pay for killing July. It didn't matter that only one bullet had killed her. Together, the killers had staged the ambush. Together, they were all responsible, and together they would all pay with their lives.

Cuno walked into the house and re-appeared on the porch a few minutes later, dressed for the trail in a broad-brimmed Stetson, fringed buckskin tunic, and red neckerchief. A pair of bulging saddlebags was slung over one shoulder; he carried a rifle and war bag in his other hand. His Colt .45 was strapped to his hip.

He set the saddlebags, war bag, and rifle in the yard, then returned to the cabin, re-appearing a moment later with a kerosene can. He poured the kerosene over the stoop and over the bodies of the two dead gun-men, which he'd dragged in earlier from the yard and the creek. He doused the two men, shook the liquid over the doorstep, then tossed the can inside.

He stood in the open doorway, looking around the small cabin in which two lanterns burned. He looked at the table and the kitchen cabinets he'd whipsawed and nailed together from pine. They weren't any-thing special, but they'd been built to last for him and July.

Only, he and July hadn't lasted, because

six men had come gunning for him, no doubt for the reward money an angry old rancher had offered for his head. Cuno knew who the man was. Cuno had killed the man's son, but the son had deserved to die. Crazed from drink, the son, Vince Evans, had been about to cut a girl's throat when Cuno had shot him.

Cuno would kill the men who'd come gunning for him, and then he'd go gunning for the man whose bounty had put them on his trail. It was a steely resolve he felt now, shouldering aside his grief enough for clear thinking, cold reasoning.

He looked around the cabin one last time, then backed off the porch, dug in his jeans pocket, and produced a match. The lucifer blazed to life on his cartridge belt. Cuno looked at it as though seeing fire for the first time, then stared at the cabin stonily, his eyes blazing in the light of the burning match.

July and the baby were dead. It seemed only fitting the farm should die too. Its presence, and all the love and hope it symbolized, only mocked him.

Let it burn.

When the match was beginning to burn his fingers, Cuno tossed it onto the stoop, turned, and began walking across the yard. The kerosene caught flame and went up in a whoosh, trailing itself like a burning snake. When it found the can inside the cabin, there was another, louder whoosh, and the windows blew out, shattering on the burning porch floor. The leaping flames licked at the eaves.

Cuno did not turn to watch. He retrieved his gear and walked over to the corral. He turned the mules loose, slapping their rumps. They'd eventually find his neighbors, who'd adopt them. As the mules thundered away from the burning cabin, he saddled his skewbald paint horse, Renegade.

When he'd touched a match to the hay in the barn, he rode stiffly out of the farmyard, the burning barn now included in the leaping, thundering fireball behind him.

His jaws and eyes were hard, though his face was still swollen from grief. His pistol was snugged up to his left hip, and his Winchester rifle jutted handily up from the rifle boot. With his broad-brimmed hat snugged down on his head, he stared straight off into the darkness — outrage and heartbreak fueling him as the beams and joists he'd erected with his own hands now fueled the conflagration behind him.

Knowing he could not track the killers until morning, he rode only a mile or so. He set up a hasty camp in a hollow and watched the sky glow above his burning farm. As he watched the flickering blush and listened to his horse idly cropping grass, he wondered if he could ever exact enough vengeance to satisfy the immensity of his loss.

Nothing short of bringing July and their baby back would do that. Nevertheless, Cuno would ride the men down and kill them without mercy, as a year ago he had ridden down and killed the two men who had butchered his father and stepmother.

He'd thought that after he married and built his farm, the world would leave him alone. That somehow God or fate or whoever was in charge of men and destinies would see that he'd been tested enough and would allow him a peaceful life with the woman he loved.

So much for the mercy of the gods. His war was far from over.

He settled back on his blankets and conjured the killers' images. He'd gotten a pretty good look at three of the four survivors. He ran those images through his mind obsessively, cementing them until, after a long time, his chin drooped. He tumbled into a restless sleep in which he dreamed he was digging a bottomless grave as July watched from above, singing her own death dirge.

He woke at the first pale of dawn, drank

water from his canteen, and choked down some jerky. When he'd saddled his horse, he traced a wide semicircle around his farm.

Mid-morning, he found fresh horse prints in a swale southwest of the burned buildings, and his heart thumped eagerly. He followed the prints closely, riding south along the rutted wagon road curving amidst the hogbacks, leaving the smoke wisps of his smoldering farm behind him.

The sun had climbed above the eastern horizon when the horse tracks brought him to the stage station nestled in a hill fold spiked with tall grass and cottonwoods. Surprised not to see smoke curling from the main building's chimney pipe, he rode into the yard. One horse — a beefy, swaybacked steeldust — stood tethered to the hitch rack before the stoop, drinking from the stock trough.

A man was bent over the well tank between the main building and the barn, splashing water on his face and naked chest. Hearing the clomp of Renegade's shod hooves, the man jerked upright and clawed at the old Remington hanging low on his thigh.

"Hold on, Sheriff," Cuno said, holding both hands shoulder-high, palms out. "It's Cuno Massey from over the bench."

The old lawman's wet-bearded, sun-seared face wrinkled as he scowled. His thin, gray-brown hair was pasted to his forehead. He was a wizened, potbellied oldster with grizzled gray chest hair gleaming wetly in the climbing sun.

He off-cocked the Remington and tipped the long barrel skyward. "Uh . . . sorry there, Massey. A little jumpy, I reckon, after what happened here."

Cuno stared hard, his face shaded by the wide brim of his Plainsman, slow to understand.

Emmet Greeley crawled back into his shirt, upon which his five-pointed sheriff's star flashed. As he buttoned the wash-worn garment, he stared back at Cuno, his expression puzzled. "I figured that's why you was here."

Quietly, his heart thudding dully, Cuno said, "What are you talking about?"

"There's been a shootin'. Ole Farley Grissom and his niece. Killed by road agents. A stage come in and found 'em both dead. The driver reported it to me in Longview. I rode out about five o'clock this mornin', buried 'em both behind the house."

Cuno's heart hammered, and his stomach rolled.

The sheriff was tucking his shirttails into

the soiled duck trousers hanging off his lean hips. "Yeah, it's a cryin' damn shame."

"How many?"

"Found six sets o' tracks. Looks like they headed east from here, along the stage trail."

"They rode east only a hundred yards or so. Then they turned north."

The sheriff stared at him. "How do you know?"

Without inflection, Cuno said, "They showed up at my place last night. They were trying to kill me. They shot my wife instead."

The sheriff's stare softened. It was several seconds before he asked, "What'd they want? Money?"

Cuno bunched his lips and fisted his hands on his thighs, fighting back his emotion. "Me."

The sheriff watched him dismount stiffly, drop Renegade's reins in the yard, and walk toward the long, low stage station. Dried, brown blood smeared the stoop before the closed door. He mounted the stoop, stepped over the blood smear, opened the door, and stared into the shadows.

Chairs and benches were overturned, as though there had been a struggle. A large pool of congealed blood lay thick near the door to the kitchen. It was smeared on an overturned chair, on a carved bird, and on an iron pot lying nearby on its side.

Cuno could smell the blood, the bodies, coppery and foul. It sickened him. He imagined Farley and Vera moving around here, working of a day, cooking and cleaning for the stage passengers. Getting along the way everyone gets along, with hard work and sweat.

Then the men who were looking for Cuno came calling, and their lives stopped here. All that was left was the animal smell of death and the bloodstains on the floor.

He heard the sheriff's soft tread on the stoop behind him.

"They shot Grissom here on the stoop. I found the niece inside. Shot twice."

Cuno nodded. His ears rang, but his expression was blank. He had few tears left to shed. Now there was only a quiet rage, a burning deep in his chest, a lingering ache in his jaws. . . .

"You know who they were?" the sheriff asked.

"Friends of a friend." Cuno swallowed back the bile in his gut and turned to face Greeley. "They probably killed Farley and Vera 'cause they wouldn't tell them where July and I lived. They knew men had come gunning for me in the past."

"Get a look at 'em?"

"I know what they look like."

The sheriff stared at him, frowning as he waited. "Well . . . ?"

Cuno walked to the edge of the stoop and blinked against the rising sun.

"Hey, I asked you a question," Greeley said, coming up behind him.

"They're mine, Sheriff," Cuno said mildly. "They're all mine."

Sheriff Greeley walked up beside Cuno, gazing at the taller, younger man skeptically. "What the hell you mean they're yours?"

Cuno stood rigidly, squinting off at the sun rising above cottonwoods by the windmill. A big crow was perched on the windmill, preening a lifted wing casually, as though everything today was the same as it had been yesterday.

"Go back home," Cuno told the aging lawman. "I'll bring them in. They'll be dead, sure as tootin', but I'll bring them in just the same."

Cuno stepped off the stoop and started walking toward his horse.

The sheriff scowled at his back. "Hey, come back here. Where you goin'?"

Cuno did not turn around as he said, "I shot two. There's four left. I'm riding them down."

"Whoa! Wait up there, boy," Greeley demanded, moving toward his horse. "I'm comin' with you."

Cuno grabbed his mount's reins and swung into the saddle. "Sorry, Sheriff. Those men killed my wife and my friends."

"Hold on, hold on," Greeley said, breathing raspily as he climbed aboard his beefy steeldust, which skittered sideways, shaking its head. "It's my job to track 'em down — not yours."

Cuno turned his horse to face Greeley. "Those men killed my wife, my unborn child, and two good friends. I'm riding them down, and I'm gonna kill them."

"I understand how you feel, son, but that's against the law."

Cuno nodded. "It's against the law, but I'm gonna do it, and no one's gonna stop me."

"Now hold on, damnit," Greeley said as he kicked his steeldust abreast of Cuno, bunching his lips angrily. "I'm the law in this county."

"Sorry, Sheriff."

"You just hold—"

Before the sheriff could finish the command, Cuno reined his horse around and gigged him into an instant gallop, sending up dust and sod gouts behind him, obscuring the sheriff's view.

69

Greeley's old mare whinnied and shied with alarm. The sheriff squinted through the dust and held tight to the reins.

"Goddamn you, you . . . *young son of a bitch!*"

Drawing the brim of his battered sugarloaf sombrero down over his forehead, he kicked the mare's flanks. Reluctantly, the steeldust skittered into a canter and then into an ambling, shuffling run.

"I'm the law here, damnit! *You'll do as I say!*"

6

Cuno rode back to where he'd left the killers' tracks, and followed them in a wide arc around the station, keeping an eye out for the sheriff. He wasn't surprised at the ease with which he'd lost the old man and the steeldust — a long-toothed mare spoiled by too many oats.

The tracks followed an ancient, deep-cut riverbed for nearly two miles. The riders had then left the cut and headed straight south, over a low bench peppered with post oaks and sage, with here and there a maverick longhorn milling in the infrequent shade or lounging around a rocky seep.

Cuno had ridden about three miles from the stage station when he reined up at the base of a rusty, scaly stone slab tilting gently down the east end of a slender mesa.

This was a dike, a volcanic ridge thrust up from below by ancient pressures. The killers had ridden up and over.

Scowling, Cuno mopped sweat from his brow.

The rocky slab was at least a hundred yards wide, which meant a hundred yards of damn hard, slow tracking. He would lose precious time scouring the rock for horse apples and shoe scrapes.

Before he had time to curse his luck, a pistol snapped.

Ducking, Cuno grabbed his Colt, holding tight to Renegade's reins as his quick eyes found the shooter. A man stood above him on the rock, about fifty yards away — a short, wiry man with a high-crowned hat.

Stiffly, bending only one knee, the man picked up something long and slender and coiling, holding it out from his body.

"Snake," Sheriff Greeley said matter-of-factly, his badge glinting in the sunlight. "I'd skin him out for lunch if I had time."

The old man holstered his gun and walked away from Cuno up the rising slope of uneven stone, a silhouetted figure diminishing against the sky, looming large and blue beyond him.

Cuno holstered his Colt and gigged the skewbald paint onto the rocky table, the shod hooves clomping loudly.

The sheriff approached a perky, long-legged bay standing hitched to its grounded reins. Cuno recognized the horse as one from Farley Grissom's stable — one of the station agent's own personally trained mounts. A well-trained mount, for that matter, as Grissom had once trained horses for the army.

Cuno's features flattened as he watched Greeley swing into the saddle. The old goat was more trouble than he looked.

"How did you know they came this way?" Cuno asked.

Greeley answered with a self-satisfied smirk. "Just a hunch. There's an old outlaw cabin — some call it a roadhouse — just south of here, and I figured maybe those long riders that ambushed you and your wife was headed that way. Sure enough, I cut the sign of four horses on the other side of this caprock."

Cuno sighed audibly. "Well, what are we waiting for?"

The sheriff beetled his gray brows. "What makes you think we're ridin' together . . . after that stunt you pulled back at the stage stop?"

Cuno shrugged. "Have it your way, Sheriff." He reined his horse south and began riding along the caprock.

"Hold on there, ye damn shavetail," the

sheriff barked behind him. He gigged his horse abreast of Cuno. "It's only out of respect for your situation I'm gonna let you tag along. Don't think for a minute I couldn't cuff you and tie you to a tree if I wanted." He leaned one arm on his saddle horn and pointed a finger threateningly. "If I can, I'm gonna take those men down alive. If you interfere, I'll jail your hide till it's fallin' off your bones. *Comprende?*"

"I hear you, Sheriff." He'd heard, all right. But one way or another, the killers would die. . . .

With a grunt, the sheriff gigged his horse over the brow of the rock and down the other side. Cuno followed suit. Silently they followed the killers' meandering trail for forty-five minutes, through hill folds, across a damp wash, and through a cottonwood copse at the edge of an old, salty lake bed. In a hollow, Greeley reined his horse to a halt, climbed out of the saddle, and shucked his Sharps rifle from its boot.

Cuno followed suit, and soon the two men were crawling on their hands and knees to the brow of a steep ridge.

In the ravine below sat a log, sod-roofed cabin patched with whipsawed boards and tar paper, washed out and gaunt in the late-morning sun. A narrow porch ran around the front and right side. On the porch were a half-dozen whiskey barrels, and a skinned antelope carcass hung from the eaves.

Adjacent to the cabin was a barn, with a collapsed roof and a corral. Five horses milled inside the corral. A dun bit a paint's ass, and a short skirmish ensued.

Regarding the cabin as he absently brushed a grasshopper from his rifle barrel, Greeley said quietly, "Lord's place stays empty for months at a time, when ole Bella's off sellin' his coffin varnish to the Injuns. But every once in a while a gang holes up here."

"Looks like one's holed up here now," Cuno said, jacking a round in his Winchester's breech. "I'll work around to the back."

"Hold on, hold on," Greeley said, grabbing his arm. "We're playin' this my way. I'm gonna ride over and pretend I'm just grublinin' through, looking for a meal and a cot for the night. I'll see if any of the men you described are inside. If not, we'll just mosey. No use causin' a hullabaloo if the men we're trailin' ain't here."

"What are you going to do if they are here?"

The sheriff cast an incredulous look at Cuno. "Arrest 'em, for chrissakes! Might as well take Lord too. There's been a federal warrant out for that old sidewinder for nigh on two months now."

With that, the sheriff scrambled back from the ridge on his knees and elbows.

"You're gonna need help."

Greeley had climbed to his knees, holding his old-model Sharps by the barrel, grinding its butt in the grass. "Son, I been a lawman these twenty years past. Started out as a Pinkerton and did a stint in the Texas Rangers. I may look a mite stove up, but you just watch an old lawdog go to work." He winked a blue eye with dogged cunning. "Maybe you'll learn somethin'."

"Learn how to get my ass shot," Cuno grumbled as the oldster climbed to his feet and ran crouching back to his horse tethered with Cuno's in a feeder ravine. But Cuno had to admit the old man had sand. He just hoped he had sense enough to realize he wasn't as young as he used to be.

A few minutes later the sheriff reappeared, in the ravine on Cuno's right, following a faint trail through the broom grass and wild currants, grasshoppers arcing around him and catching the bold sunshine. The sheriff had removed his badge. He rode lazily in the saddle — just a lonely, aging saddle tramp who'd come a long way and had happened onto a cabin.

Cuno felt a nerve jump in his temple as he

76

watched the sheriff walk the bay up to the roadhouse.

The nerve in Cuno's temple picked up its twitching. The cabin was too quiet. He squeezed his Winchester's stock, fingered the trigger. But at a good hundred yards from the cabin, he was too far away to do much if Greeley got into trouble. If he moved now, he might be seen.

In the ravine, the sheriff approached the cabin, cast his gaze about while maintaining a neutral expression. There was no sound but the wind ruffling the grass and causing the shack's weathered timbers to creak. Bob-whites flitted in the tall weeds, and the five horses in the corral watched the lawman gravely.

The latch clicked; the timbered door squeaked slowly open. A man appeared in the opening — tall with thin, gray hair pulled back in a ponytail and a round face with hard, slanted eyes. He wore baggy denims held up with rawhide galluses bowing out from his paunch. An English-style revolver protruded from his waistband. Greeley had never met Bella Lord, but he'd heard him described and seen his etching on wanted dodgers.

"That's far enough there, fella," Lord said in a womanish, high-pitched voice.

Greeley reined his bay to a halt. He nodded. "Howdy-do. Name's Green. Was wonderin' if you could spare a cup of coffee, maybe a plate of beans, or just some pan bread." The old sheriff smiled affably. "I'm so damn hungry my gizzard's startin' to think my throat's takin' a vacation."

The old gent with the ponytail studied him narrow-eyed. He looked behind the sheriff, cutting his eyes from side to side, sweeping the distance, working his lips suspiciously.

Returning his small-eyed gaze to Greeley, he said, sneering, "Cup of coffee and a plate of beans, eh?" Lord growled around a sneer. "What's this look like — friggin' Delmonico's?"

Greeley shrugged. He tried to look around Lord into the cabin, but the man's bulk filled the door. The sheriff smiled agreeably, his chest muscles taut and his fingers tingling with contained excitement. Here stood the infamous Bella Lord. Goddamn.

Greeley lowered his eyes and shifted his feet, truckling. "If no, then I reckon I'll ride on."

Lord studied Greeley skeptically for a long time, a mocking smile on his smooth, fleshy face in which two, crazy blue eyes resided deep in doughy sockets. Finally, he tipped his head to one side. "You sure that's all you're lookin' for?"

"That's all," Greeley said, shrugging. He fashioned a guileless smile, glancing at the two front windows for movement.

Lord squinted his eyes skeptically. "You sure you ain't a lawman? One of them tin stars from one of the settlements" — he scrunched up his face — "lookin' for *outlaws?*"

The sheriff smiled as though flattered. "Now, do I look like a lawman to you?"

Lord frowned, canted his head to the other side. He dropped his eyes to the old Remington on Greeley's hip. Apparently satisfied the sheriff was who he said he was, the man grumbled, "Me and the boys done had lunch, but you can heat up some beans, I reckon. Then vamoose. I don't cotton to strangers."

"Obliged." Greeley started climbing out of his saddle. He chuckled. "Hell, I been without a meal for so long, my belly's startin' to think my throat's been cut!"

From the ridge above the ravine, Cuno watched the sheriff climb down from the saddle and amble nonchalantly over to the hitching post.

Movement to the right of the cabin caught Cuno's eye. A horse and rider were trotting toward the cabin, descending a low rise, the man's rifle butt snugged against his belt. The barrel, leveled at Greeley, flashed in the sun.

A drum beat in Cuno's chest, and his throat went dry.

Greeley heard the man before he saw him.

"Don't let him in, Bella," the rifleman called, his voice tense as piano wire, harsh with warning. "I was huntin' above the ridge when I seen him and another hombre ride this way. This man here was wearin' a sheriff's star."

Greeley had paused with one boot on the cabin's stoop.

"You don't friggin' say," said Lord, grinning. His hand moved to his pistol butt.

Greeley's heart tumbled. He looked at Lord. Slowly, he turned his head back to the tall man in the Texas hat riding toward him on a zebra dun. The man raised his rifle to his shoulder. The bore yawned wide at Greeley's head.

"Shit, shit, shit," Cuno said on the ridge above the ravine, extending his rifle and lowering his head to the stock, sighting down the barrel. He shifted the bead to the rider approaching the cabin, but the man was merely a wavering, featureless silhouette from this distance.

Cuno had little chance of hitting his target. Even if he did, the man on the stoop would take out Greeley with the revolver stuffed in his pants.

The next few seconds passed as if in a dream. Cuno bounded to his feet, scampering, half-falling down the ridge to the ravine, running toward the cabin, yelling, "Hold it, you sons o' bitches!"

As his boots pummeled the sod beneath him, the horseman's rifle puffed smoke, the fluting bark echoing a second later as Greeley twirled, clutching his chest, falling back onto the stoop and rolling off under the alarmed bay's twisting, shaking head and prancing feet.

The rider swung down from his saddle, jerked around toward Cuno, and dropped to a knee. Lord bounded off the stoop in an awkward, shuffling gait, his ponytail bouncing on his shoulder. He produced his pistol from his pants. Cuno spied movement in the doorway — another man emerging from the cabin. Then he saw that the rifleman was planting a bead on him. He stopped and threw himself to his right, hitting the ground on his shoulder.

The rifleman's gun barked, and Cuno felt the slug's path a few inches above his head. He was about to return fire, but instinct told him to roll left, and two shots — one from the rifleman and one from the old man — sliced the air to his right.

He rolled once more, avoiding another of the old man's shots, lined up the bead at the end of his barrel with the back sight, planting them both squarely on the still-kneeling rifleman, and squeezed the trigger.

The Winchester jumped and belched smoke, and the rifleman tipped right, dropping his rifle and grabbing his right shoulder. Hearing the wounded man's muffled curse, Cuno rolled back to his right, avoiding two more shots from the old man.

On his elbows once again, Cuno fired at Lord. The shot sailed wide and plunked into the cabin. Lord trotted awkwardly, his protruding gut, jowls, and gray ponytail bouncing, toward Cuno. He stopped, planted his front foot, and fired, the lead resounding off a rock near Cuno's right boot.

Cuno levered and fired, levered and fired. Lord went down screaming as holes sprouted blood from his face and throat, triggering his last slug skyward.

He hit the ground in a heap, arched his back, and snapped down, dead.

"Son of a bitch!" yelled the dark, hawk-faced young man who was holding his right shoulder with his left hand and crawling toward his rifle.

Cuno glanced around for the man he'd seen leaving the cabin behind Lord, then shuttled his gaze back to the rifleman. "Grab that Winchester and die!"

Heedless of the warning, the man grabbed the rifle in his left arm, planted the butt, and awkwardly jacked a shell in the chamber one-handed. He hadn't dropped the barrel six inches before Cuno shot him, planting him on his back with a clipped wail.

Looking around through his powder smoke for the third man, Cuno whipped his head from left to right. Neither of the two men he'd killed were part of the bunch he was looking for. Hoping the third man was, Cuno thumbed fresh cartridges into his rifle, then jacked a fresh round into the breach. He yelled, "Come on out here and face me, you yellow son of a bitch!"

A woman's voice answered, muffled by the wind. "He ain't in here, mister. Please don't shoot. It's just me in here! Everybody else left!"

Cuno squinted his eyes at the cabin, watching for movement. "Where's Page Hudson?"

"How the hell should I know? He and his boys left just after dawn."

Cuno climbed to a knee. He was catty-corner to the cabin, able to see the front as well as the entire west side, shaded slightly by the overhanging roof and sagging lengths of dead sod. He stood cautiously and, hunkered over the rifle extended from his right hip, moved toward the cabin.

From around back, footsteps rose. A man appeared, running toward an overturned farm wagon sheathed in ruffling wild oats. Cuno dropped to his knees as the half-dressed man in a floppy hat fired two pistol shots. When the man ducked behind the wagon, Cuno lifted his rifle and fired until five empty casings lay smoking at his feet, and the man behind the wagon was screaming.

Cuno ran toward the wagon, bolted around it, and brought the Winchester to bear. The gunman was down on his back, clutching his neck, from which blood geysered. Another hole shone low in his right side, and another gleamed wetly in his cheek.

Face twisted with pain, the outlaw stared up at Cuno beseechingly. Cuno gazed back at him, heartless. The cool precision had returned to him, the same calm born of a deep fury that had made it possible for him, just a tinhorn younker a year ago, to have trained himself to kill and to have stalked and killed his father's and stepmother's killers. The same fury was back now, and with it had returned — from where, he had no idea — his nerveless, shameless, thoughtless ability.

Apparently, it was like the ability to breathe. Once you had the ability to kill, it did not leave you. His joy, his compassion, his zest for the simple things in life — all were gone within only a few horrible hours.

Complying with the man's silent plea, Cuno put his rifle up to the man's forehead and fired. Without bothering to look at his handiwork, he regarded the cabin gravely. Although none of the men here were of the group he was looking for, he wasn't sorry he'd killed them. They were all cut from the same cloth.

Just the same, Greeley had died foolishly, for nothing. And the Hudson gang was several long hours ahead of Cuno.

Footsteps sounded, crunching grass. A fleshy blonde wearing too much face paint appeared around a corner of the cabin. Her features were drawn, her eyes timid and fearful as she studied the young stranger. His face was broad, clean, unlined, with fair skin tanned by the sun. It was a face that seemed hardly touched by the chill fates and the sins of other men. It was not the face of a killer.

Yet it was. . . .

Her painted cheeks rose with incredulity

as she studied him further. His flat, hard eyes seemed to belong to another person, a seasoned frontiersman or a long rider . . . the man who'd killed these men . . .

"Who are you anyway?" she heard herself ask.

7

Marcella Jiminez galloped the pinto pony up a barren shelf, reined the horse to a halt, and swung her gaze around anxiously, her long hair flying out from her shoulders.

Under the brim of her man's felt hat, her brows furrowed and her full lips stretched a grimace. Nervously, she fingered the small Smith & Wesson she carried in her waistband — a gun she'd stolen off a drunk miner who'd tried to drag her into an abandoned mine shaft in Bisbee.

She wore a green plaid shirt beneath the vest and blue Levi's stuffed into low-heeled black boots. It was comfortable riding garb, with the added benefit of making her look like a man from a distance, saving her from lonely, randy riders looking for a woman to use.

The gambler, whom she had known little more than a month, had bought her the pinto from a Comanche half-breed in

Nacogdoches. The horse had a wild air and a reckless light in its eyes, which made it and Marcella a fitting match. Marcella Jiminez was no hothouse flower. A girl who'd been struggling for survival since the day she'd left her tiny Sonoran village when she was thirteen, she had little time for niceties — unless they put money in her pocket, a roof over her head, or food in her mouth.

Practicality was the name of her game.

She reined the horse in a circle, muttering Spanish curses and searching the landscape with her large, liquid-brown eyes, the center of her full upper lip curling back upon itself, as it had a tendency to do when she was pensive or angry, driving weaker men to lusty, oafish distraction.

It was the Hudson gang she was looking for now.

Where were they? Where in hell were they?

Earlier, she'd waited in her bed until Hudson and the other three men had left the roadhouse. Then she'd gotten up, dressed quickly, saddled the pinto, and ridden after them. Her intention was to follow the four men as closely as she could without being seen. She'd wait until they'd bedded down for the night, then she'd steal into their camp, shoot all three while they slept, and confiscate the map.

To that end, she'd ridden hard, harder than the tracks of Hudson and his men had indicated they had ridden. But then she'd lost the trail about an hour ago, in a brushy ravine, and try as she had, she could not get it back.

"Mierda," she muttered.

Should she swing back and follow her own trail until it intersected theirs again? Or should she continue southwest and hope she overran their sign accidentally?

Her uncertainty and sudden sense of aloneness out here in these barren wastes made her belly raw and her breath short. She hadn't paid much attention to the way she'd come — only the way she was going. She doubted she'd be able to find her way back to the roadhouse. Trying to find it might only carry her into Indian country, but it was her only option.

She did not want to lose time backtracking her own trail. She wanted to catch up to the riders before dark. After dark, she'd retrieve the map and be on her way. But only after shooting Page Hudson through his savage heart and watching him squirm and kick in his blankets as his blood poured out on the ground.

The memory of him plucking the map from her mother's crucifix with mocking smugness stiffened her back and ground her molars. She could still smell his fetid breath blowing in her face as he pounded away between her legs, rubbing her breasts raw with his unshaven cheeks and callused hands. The recollection flooded her stomach with angry bile, curled the rose-petal nub of her pretty upper lip.

She regretted luring him back to her bed. She'd intended to allow him to make love to her, but Page Hudson did not know how to make love. He had raped her.

She looked around again, regaining her resolve and adjusting the thonged felt hat on her head. She gigged the pinto down off the rimrock and onto a game trail meandering through rusty buttes.

In the far distance were low, green mountains. The town was probably there, at the base of the mountains.

She'd head toward them. That was where those greasy gringos were heading. She'd bet her life on it.

Cuno stood over Greeley's twisted, bloody body before the roadhouse. With a fateful sigh, he leaned down, grabbed the body under its arms, and gently dragged it to the south edge of the yard. Finding a shovel in the barn, he dug a shallow grave, eased the sheriff inside, and covered him.

He regretted not taking the time to dig a deeper hole. The old lawman deserved a decent burial. But Cuno didn't have time. Hudson was ahead and gaining ground fast.

Cuno turned to the blonde, who'd been watching him from the porch, feathers sagging in her hair. "Will you send word about the sheriff to Denby?"

The blonde shrugged and nodded.

Leaving the dead outlaws where he'd shot them, Cuno forked leather and cantered out of the weed-grown yard, following the five sets of fresh horse prints that emerged from the corral and swung south and west.

He didn't pay much attention to the fact that there were five sets of tracks instead of just four. Apparently, the killers had picked up another man. It didn't matter to Cuno. Five was only one more than four, and any man riding with the killers was guilty by association.

The tracks didn't follow a road, because there weren't many roads in this remote corner of the territory. The riders' sign rose and fell over the hogbacks, skirting rimrocks and buttes, marking the mud along seeps where the men had paused to water their mounts and fill their canteens.

Cuno rode hard, grimly determined. But

the riders' trail was difficult to follow over stony riverbeds and rocky shelves, and several times he lost it and wasted precious time retrieving it. His heart wrenched and his gut tightened at the thought of losing the trail for good — of July's killers riding free.

When he'd crossed a large talus patch around the base of a rimrock, he saw that one of the five riders had broken away from the group. Wary of a possible ambush, Cuno looked around carefully, made sure he wasn't in a dry-gulcher's sights, and rode on.

Later, ascending another in an endless monotony of low hills spiked with bunchgrass and sage, he drew Renegade up short. He fingered the butt of his .45 as he cast his gaze left. Something had flashed out there, about a hundred yards east — like the sun's reflection off a saddle cinch or a rifle barrel.

"Gidup, horse!" he commanded, bulling Renegade down the other side of the knoll, through shrubs and into an arroyo. Reining the horse to a halt, he slipped out of the saddle and quickly wrapped the reins around a cottonwood.

He shucked his Winchester and trotted east through the arroyo. He followed the old creek bed for seventy yards. When he came to a bend, he stepped around it slowly, his rifle held before him in both hands.

Around the bend, a stream entered the ravine from the south, curving into a wide, green canyon. Deep in the willows along the stream stood a pinto pony with a star-shaped dapple on its snout, only its head visible above the breeze-buffeted brush. The horse looked toward Cuno, and Cuno crouched down. When he straightened a moment later, the horse had lowered its head again.

Cuno ran crouching into the willows. He walked through them slowly, quietly until he heard the stream murmuring and the horse munching grass only a few feet to his right.

A few more steps brought him to the water's edge. He set his jaws and brought the rifle to his shoulder. Staring straight ahead, he froze.

Before him, a woman knelt on a damp-brown sandbar — a young woman with long, chestnut hair. She wore blue jeans and men's low-heeled riding boots, and that was nearly all. Her white chemise hung down her slender, golden arms as she cupped water to her face, to her long, slender neck, and to her naked breasts jutting and bobbing over the water as she moved. Her brown nipples pebbled and jutted sensuously at the water's cool caress.

As he watched her, Cuno's knees ached;

his throat went tight and dry. The rifle sagged in his arms.

It was July.

July was kneeling there, washing in Johnson Creek only a few yards behind the cabin. She scooped water to her face and chest, caressing her naked skin with a cool, moist bandanna. Her damp hair glistened in the sun, clung to her shoulders and breasts. This girl looked so much like Cuno's young, dead wife that he began forming her name with his lips. Before he could make a sound, however, the girl looked up suddenly.

Seeing him, she screamed and bolted to her feet. She turned to run, but tripped over a rock, fell, and froze, terror etched in her wide, brown eyes. Awkwardly, she climbed to her knees and drew her chemise over her breasts.

"Who the hell are you!" she yelled with a heavy Spanish accent. "And what the hell are you doing — watching a girl bathe? Were you raised by jackals?"

Cuno stumbled backward, jolted from his reverie. "I'm sorry . . . thought you were someone else."

He followed her darting glance to the shore. A few feet to his left lay a green plaid shirt and a Smith & Wesson pocket revolver with cracked grips and a rusty barrel. Walk-

94

ing over, he picked up the shirt.

"Here," he said, tossing it to her. She could retrieve the gun herself, after he was safely out of range.

She snapped the shirt out of the air with one hand.

"Hasta luego." He turned, started away, and remembering that one rider had separated from the group he was after, stopped. Turning back to her, he said, "You wouldn't be traveling with four men, would you? The four that passed near here a couple hours ago?"

Marcella studied the big young man with shaggy, blond hair hanging down from his wide-brimmed Plainsman hat. He cut an impressive figure, to which the bullet graze high on his right cheek added a dangerous aspect. But she wasn't thinking so much about him as Hudson.

Apparently, she hadn't been far off the gringo cutthroat's trail. What was this hombre doing on it? Marcella figured he wasn't much older than she was, and he didn't look like a lawman. He wore no badge on the fringed, buckskin tunic straining across his shoulders. He appeared capable and tough enough for the owlhoot trail, but something in his eyes told her he wasn't an outlaw.

Offering no reply to his question, she

merely stared at him, pensively curling her lip.

He stared back at her. She felt herself shrink slightly from the animosity hardening his blue eyes, a look that made her wonder if he wasn't an outlaw after all.

"You with them?" he asked again, with a menacing edge in his voice.

"I am not *with* them," she said haughtily. "I am following them."

"Why?"

She furled her brows. "You ask a lot of questions for someone who sneaks up on bathing women!"

"Never mind," he said impatiently, turning again and walking back through the brush.

She stared after him, confounded by the abruptness of his departure. "Wait!" she called behind him. "Wait for me!"

Cuno continued walking back the way he'd come, impatient to get after the killers. Hearing her calling and running up behind him, he turned. She'd donned her shirt but had left it unbuttoned, holding it closed with her left hand while carrying her gun, butt-forward, in her right.

"You are tracking Hudson?" She didn't wait for his reply. "Let me ride with you."

Cuno frowned skeptically. "Why?"

"He stole something from me. Something that belonged to my family," she lied.

Cuno's skeptical frown remained on his rawboned features, furrowing his sun-bleached brows. He shook his head and began walking away.

She ran after him, grabbed his arm. Breathless, she beseeched him. "Please. You are after them, I am after Hudson. You can track them, yes, but I know where they are going."

He looked down at her, wondering if she was telling the truth. Knowing where the killers were heading would save him considerable time.

"If you know where they're headin'," he said, cocking a skeptical brow, "why do you need to track 'em?"

"Because I do not know where I am. But I know where they are going."

"Where?"

"Ha!" She laughed without mirth. "If I told you, you would leave me. I will tell you when we are close."

"Maybe I don't give a shit where they're going," Cuno growled. "If I can shake loose of you, I might be able to catch up to them before nightfall."

She shook her head. "They are farther ahead of you than that. I may not be much of a tracker, but I know their trail is several hours old. They left the roadhouse early this morning. One rainstorm" — she glanced at the blue sky and snapped her fingers — "and you've lost their trail forever!"

Marcella narrowed her eyes at him haughtily. She did not know why he was after Hudson, and she didn't care. All she cared about was the gold. She doubted this young, handsome stranger, capable as he appeared, could kill Hudson. But he could probably track him, and that was all Marcella needed. She'd take over from there, though she hadn't yet determined how.

She stared up at his implacable, suntanned face. He regarded her thoughtfully, lines of indecision etched across his forehead. If she really did know where Hudson was headed, he thought he could probably beat it out of her. The problem was he'd never lifted a hand against a woman, and he doubted he could do it now, even for July.

She shrugged, canted her head coquettishly while loosening her grip on her shirt, flashing a good portion of one breast and all but the nipple of the other. "Later, I can make up for any inconvenience. . . . "

She flashed him again.

He scowled and turned away, snarling, "Keep your shirt on, lady, and get your damn horse."

It wasn't much over two minutes before Cuno was back on the killers' trail, the girl and her pinto following close behind. Cuno could ride only so fast without losing the sign in a talus slide or on a gravelly bench; he had to go slow and keep an eye peeled on the ground beneath his horse's hooves.

He cursed the time he'd lost messing with the girl, whose name he'd learned during a spurt of intermittent conversation.

As they rode, he tried to convince her to tell him Hudson's destination, but received nothing in reply but snooty silence. She did tell him the names of the men he was after, however. Hudson and Saber were the only two he'd heard of. They were stage robbers who'd moved into the country from the Southwest, where the Texas and Arizona Rangers had turned up the heat.

Cuno had heard the names mentioned in warning, as in: "Careful out there — Hudson's boys are on the cold-steel prowl."

Cuno figured Hudson had gotten tired of robbing stagecoaches and raping female passengers; he'd probably gotten wind of the bounty on Cuno's head, heard Cuno was farming in the area, and decided to try his hand at head-hunting.

But why had he given up so easily? He'd

lost only two men. The four could have returned to the farm later, after they'd planned better, and staged another ambush. Outlaws were generally cocky and determined, with an exaggerated sense of their abilities. Cuno was just one man against four.

Since Hudson's men hadn't returned, and since they were hastily moving south, there had to be something luring them in that direction. Something worth more money than the bounty on Cuno's head.

Something they'd learned about at the roadhouse . . .

Cuno glanced at the girl riding behind him, sitting her saddle with regal stiffness, frowning and holding her reins up close to her chest, upper lip curled back upon itself. She probably knew. But her knowing and her telling were two different things altogether.

Cuno didn't really care what was drawing Hudson south. All he cared about was catching up to him and his companions, and filling them all with lead.

A moment later, when horses plunged down a low ridge to his and the girl's right, he thought his opportunity was at hand. Hooves thundered, stones clattered, dust rose. Then, through the sifting dust, he saw three bare-chested Indians smeared with war paint.

His stomach sank. His hand froze on his holstered Colt.

As the ponies halted before him, the Indians faced him, naked chests glistening, rifles in their hands, dark challenge in their eyes.

8

Drawing his horse up short, Cuno touched his .45 but left the gun in its holster. All three Indians had their rifles pointed at his head, daring him to draw.

Beside him, the girl gasped but fought her frightened horse under control. Cuno was impressed by her relative calm.

"Easy," he encouraged her in a low, even voice. "Just take it nice and easy."

Where had the redskins come from all of a sudden? They must have spied him and the girl from a long ways off and laid up in those crevices above the trail, waiting.

By the way he carried himself, the Indian in the middle of the group, riding a tall, black stardust stallion, was apparently their leader. He had a round, flat face with a yellow front tooth protruding over his chapped bottom lip. A bandolier crossed his right shoulder, and the carbine in his hands was an old, single-shot Krag.

Leaning forward on his horse's bare back, he barked his guttural tongue. Cuno met the leader's glare, his expression neutral. Frustrated, the young brave extended an arm and jutted a finger at Renegade and the girl's pinto, and then at Marcella herself, spitting his unintelligible demands once again.

"Savages," Marcella hissed.

"You know what he's saying?"

"He's saying they want our horses . . . and me," the girl said in a voice pinched with as much disdain as fear.

The bucktoothed brave continued spitting and pointing.

Cuno turned to the girl and raised his eyebrows.

She narrowed her eyes at him but didn't say anything.

"What'd he say?" Cuno growled with impatience.

"He says if you give them me and the horses, they'll let you pass unharmed." She raised a challenging brow.

Cuno stared at the three braves. They stared back at him, but they were obviously more interested in the girl. They shuttled their lascivious gazes down her body and back up again, black eyes bright with anticipation.

"Sure would make things easy," Cuno said.

"My knight in shining armor," she growled.

Cuno sighed and shifted around in his saddle. "Yeah."

He wondered why they didn't just shoot him and take what they wanted. Who knows what goes through the mind of an Indian? Maybe they'd gain more honor by setting him afoot, which, out here, would be the same thing as killing him anyway.

"Well?" the girl demanded, the fear in her eyes belying her challenging tone.

Appraising the braves' old-model rifles, all of which were single-shots, Cuno asked her if she spoke Comanche.

Marcella shook her head. "I understand a little, like everyone else in northern Mejico."

The Indians had lowered their rifles and relaxed in their saddles, smiling, enjoying the fear they sensed.

"When I give the word," Cuno said quietly, "drop out of your saddle and cover your head."

She looked at him, frowning, lip curling. "What?"

"Just do it."

Cuno leaned forward over Renegade's mane and made a sideways slashing motion with his hand.

"No!" he raged. "You can't have horses, you can't have girl. You try for them and you die!"

All three braves stared hard at him now, stunned, jaws set with mute exasperation. Cuno kept his eyes on the leader, but he knew the tall, skinny savage on the leader's right would make the first move. He sensed it, read it in the brave's quick eyes.

He was right. In the periphery of his vision he saw the skinny brave's Spencer tighten in his arms, the barrel yawning.

"Drop!" Cuno yelled at the girl.

Moving quickly, not thinking but only re-acting to the threat and to the sudden flashes of movement he sensed as much as saw, Cuno ducked and spun Renegade in a tight circle as the skinny brave air-whipped a bul-let over his left ear. Cuno clawed his Colt .45 from the cross-draw holster and shot the brave off his horse.

Reining Renegade to the right, making a moving target for the other two Comanches, he fired two quick shots over Renegade's bobbing head. The first slug took the leader through his right shoulder. The brave sagged back while Cuno's Colt popped again, in time with the third brave's carbine.

He didn't wait to make certain he'd hit the brave before turning again to the bucktoothed leader, who was struggling with his horse and screaming, *"Ay-eeeee!"*

As the leader brought the Spencer around weakly, trying feebly to take aim at Cuno, Cuno shot him through the left eye, blood and gray matter spraying out behind the brave's head, painting his horse's ass with gore.

The third brave was on the ground, climbing to his knees, dripping blood from a wound just above his right hip. Cuno gigged Renegade over and leaned down as the Indian looked up, raking a knife from his belt scabbard. Cuno set the Colt's barrel against the brave's head and pulled the trigger.

The brave's head blew sideways in a spray of blood, his body crumpling, the Spencer dropping. "I'm bettin' you wish your proddy leader had taken my advice," Cuno said.

Cuno gigged Renegade forward and whipped around. The skinny brave lay facedown between two pink rocks. His right foot moved and his back rose and fell sharply. Calmly, Cuno extended the Colt, aiming at the back of the brave's head, and fired.

The brave stiffened and relaxed after the foot gave a final kick.

Renegade whinnied. Cuno spun him again, looking around. The Indians' horses were galloping off down the canyon, dust sifting in their wake. Renegade blew nervously, straining against the reins held taut in Cuno's gloved hands. The horse had smelled blood before — plenty of it — but it had been a while.

Marcella crouched near a rock, gazing up between the elbows shielding her head. Her horse too was gone. When the shooting had started, it had run back the way she and Cuno had come.

"It's all right," Cuno said now, running his eyes along the low, rocky ridge from which the three Comanches had appeared, not seeing any more. "I think. . . ."

Marcella stared up at Cuno, who remained in his saddle as the dust sifted over him, flouring his hat and shoulders. His Colt was still in his hand, held low near his thigh, smoke curling from the barrel.

She blinked her eyes and slowly lowered her arms, her eyes on the young man on the skewbald paint, her expression betraying her amazement at the young drifter's talent for killing.

"Shake a leg," he told her, jerking her up by her arm. "We gotta find your horse and get movin'."

That night the killers of July Massey camped in a canyon roughly eight miles ahead of Cuno and Marcella. After it was good dark, big Clevis O'Malley entered the sphere of firelight carrying an armload of wood he'd gleaned from a wash.

He dropped the whole load on the guttering fire and stepped back from the flying cinders.

"Jesus H. Christ!" Page Hudson yelled, lifting an arm to cover his face. He sat with his back to a tree only a few feet from the fire ring. "What the hell you think you're doin', Clevis?"

"You told me to get more wood, didn't ye?"

"I didn't tell you to throw the whole works on the fire!" Hudson brushed white ashes from the map he'd stolen from Marcella Jiminez. He'd been studying the map when Clevis had thrown the wood on the fire. "You burn a hole through my map, and I'm gonna blow a hole through you."

"You and your goddamn map," O'Malley snarled. "I'd bet pennies to army hardtack it leads right to an empty hole."

"Why do you say that, Cleve?" Kenny Wilks asked with characteristic mildness.

He was sitting on a log, back a ways from the fire, changing the bandage on his wounded arm. His canteen was open beside him. The wound had turned out to be little more than a graze, but Kenny's father and two cousins had died from infections, and his brother had lost an arm when, after he was scratched during a knife fight, gangrene had set in. Kenny was taking no chances. He'd taken a sheet from the roadhouse and had cut it up into enough bandage-sized strips for a nightly change for the next two weeks.

"Treasure maps always lead to wild-goose chases," Clevis said. "Everybody knows that."

"Ain't no treasure map ever led me on no wild-goose chase," Billy Saber said.

The willowy hard case probed the fire with a stick, gathering the new branches in a neat pile at which a growing flame licked. In his free hand he held a whiskey bottle by its neck. He was wobbly on his feet, and his voice was thick.

Hudson didn't mind the man's drinking. Billy had killed more men when he was drunk than when he was sober. Somehow, alcohol seemed to calm his nerves and steady his aim.

"In fact," Saber added, poking the glowing stick at Clevis, "I once followed a treasure map my ownself. Found it on a miner I killed. The map led me to a buried cigar box where the son of a bitch had stashed thirty-seven dollars."

"Thirty-seven dollars!" O'Malley intoned, grabbing his chest. "Cease this excitement. My heart can't take it!"

Kenny Wilks laughed his falsetto laugh, rocking the shabby bowler on his head.

Hudson carefully folded the map and returned it to his boot. His voice was tense and sarcastic. "If you don't want to come, vamoose! We don't need you — do we, boys?"

O'Malley looked around at the others. Wilks shrugged.

Saber grinned his gap-toothed grin, the brim of his gray forage hat pushed high. "Hell, no, we don't need this corkhead."

O'Malley turned to Hudson tensely. "We shoulda gone back and finished what we started with that Massey kid. His head's worth three thousand dollars. *Sure* dollars. This treasure trail we're on is a long one, through some of the most woolly country in the Southwest. And I still ain't convinced there's gold at the end of it. Your brother mighta just drawed this map to throw you off his trail. Hell, maybe that girl just planted a fake map to fool you. Maybe she's got all that gold hid herself somewhere."

Hudson snorted. "If Marcella has the gold, what in the hell was she doing at Bella Lord's roadhouse?"

O'Malley lifted a shoulder. "Maybe she

110

spent it already. You know what spendthrifts women are. You said she was a whore. Well, whores are even worse."

"That ain't always true," Kenny Wilks offered.

He was carefully wrapping his arm, an awkward maneuver using only his right hand. He'd asked for help, but the others had scoffed, refusing. "I once knew a whore in Wichita that was tighter'n the bark on a tree. She'd suffered through some mighty lean times, and she knew money wasn't always easy to come by. Why, if she needed curtains for her cabin —"

"Ah, shut up, Kenny!" Hudson said. "Shut up and finish wrapping your goddamn arm and be done with it."

"Hey, Kenny," Billy Saber said, looking at Wilks strangely. "Your color ain't good."

Wilks was worried. "What do you mean my color ain't good?"

"Look at him, boys," Saber said. "You ever seen such a sickly-lookin' mug?"

"Why, he does look a mite froggy, now that you mention it," Hudson agreed, canting his head and squinting his eyes around the fire. "Kinda green- and yellow-lookin' around the eyes."

"Green and yellow?" Wilks asked, paling. He touched his cheek with his fingertips probingly. "Green and yellow?"

"Oh, Jesus!" Saber cried, clapping his hands to his horse-ugly face, twisted with mock horror. "It's blood poisonin', Kenny! We're gonna have to chop your arm off!"

"Oh, shut up, Billy!" Wilks said. "For Christ's sake, quit foolin' around!"

"Ah, shit!" O'Malley said. He'd had his fill of these chickenshits, who'd rather chase a pot of gold than some kid who'd proven himself handy with a rifle. With another curse, he lumbered off in search of more wood.

Around the fire, Wilks, Saber, and Hudson sat in thoughtful silence. Finally, Saber sleeved his nose and said with a confessional air, "If you say there's gold, Page, then I figure there's gold. No question."

"Good," Hudson said as he produced his fixings bag from his shirt pocket and began rolling a smoke. "Because there is. My brother didn't have time to spend it, and he drew that map for himself, for after he got shed of me. Only he didn't get shed of me."

Hudson grinned eerily as he sprinkled tobacco on wheat paper. "I caught up to the sumbitch north of Tucson and tortured him — cut off both ears and carved his face up real good. Somewheres in there he confessed he'd stashed the gold in rough country, hopin' I'd believe Indians had taken it from him after we'd split up to get shed of a posse."

Hudson licked the quirley closed and struck a match on his boot, lighting up. "He also confessed to havin' drawn a map to the place he stashed it — the fool had the memory of a blond-headed whore. When I got him to tell me what he done with the map, I cut his throat. Figured it'd be easier to follow a map than to get him, bleedin' dry as he was, to give me accurate directions."

Hudson shook his head at the folly of his decision.

"He hid it in the bean-eater bitch's crucifix?" Saber asked.

Hudson glanced at him reprovingly. "Now, don't call her a bitch, Billy. That bean-eater was almost my sister-in-law, for chrissakes."

"Sorry."

"Yeah, in the crucifix. Figured it'd be the last place anyone would look, includin' her." Hudson drew deep on the yellow cigarette and shook his head again. Releasing the smoke through his nostrils, he said in a low, grim voice, "I spent two months looking for that little whore. Finally gave her up for dead. Marcella's kind don't live to be very long in the tooth."

"How come Rick didn't tell her?" Kenny Wilks asked. He'd finished wrapping his arm and was moving it carefully up and down, testing his strength. His shabby suit coat was stained with dried blood.

"Because Rick didn't trust her." Hudson licked the quirley closed, shaking his head sadly. "Ain't that a shame — a man not trusting his own fiancée not to rob him? It's one thing not to trust your brother — Rick and me never was close — but the woman you'd asked to be your wife?" He scratched a lucifer alight on his belt buckle. "That's a cryin' shame."

Kenny Wilks sighed and looked around. "What are we gonna do about Apaches and whatnot?"

"What's that?" Hudson said, blowing cigarette smoke at the fire.

"Hell, we're headin' straight into 'Pache country. . . ."

Billy Saber tittered as he ran an oily cloth over his pistol.

"Well, we are, ain't we?" Wilks said, his anger aroused once again. Why was he always the one to ask reasonable questions, only to get laughed at for his good sense?

"Ah, shut up, Kenny," Hudson said, sucking on his quirley.

But Wilks had a point. That was why Hudson had told his partners about the map and the gold. He needed them to help him fetch the cache out of Indian country, where Rick had hidden it from the lawmen salting his trail as well as from his brother, whom he'd double-crossed. Hudson doubted he could survive the trip alone. No one traveled alone in Indian country — and lived to tell about it, that is.

You needed at least three men. Four was even better.

Yep, four.

Suddenly realizing he needed O'Malley, who'd hunted Apache scalps along the Mexican border, Hudson stood with a sigh and headed off in the direction of the big Irishman. He heard the hollow thuds of branches knocking together, and called, "Cleve. Cleve, old boy, where in the hell are ye?"

O'Malley grunted about fifty feet away. Brush thrashed. Hudson moved toward the sounds, finding O'Malley with another armload of wood and making his way back to the campfire, bulling through the greasewood and bunchgrass.

"Hey, what are you workin' so hard for?" Hudson said, manufacturing a friendly tone. "We got all the wood we're gonna need for tonight. Why don't you settle down and let me give you a drink? You deserve a drink

115

after all the wood you gathered."

"Someone had to gather it," O'Malley carped. "I'm the errand boy, ain't I?"

"Come on, Cleve," Hudson said, slapping a hand on the big man's thick shoulder. "You ain't no errand boy."

"Yeah? Try tellin' that to Wilks and Saber. They don't do shit but eat and drink once we set up camp. They don't think about things like . . ."

His voice trailed off when he saw Hudson standing before him, smoking and grinning.

"What the hell's the matter with you?" O'Malley asked suspiciously.

"Twenty-five thousand dollars is the matter with me, Cleve. Twenty-five thousand. That's why I called off the Massey hunt. It's there, Cleve."

"Oh, yeah?"

"I ever lied to you before? Didn't I get you away from that worthless Davidson gang and set you on the path of *real* fun?"

Holding his load of wood, O'Malley fidgeted, looking around.

"Has any stage we ever robbed had anything less than five hundred dollars in the strongbox?"

O'Malley didn't say anything.

"Has any whore I ever promised you been anything but a top-notch thumper?"

O'Malley shrugged. "Well . . . no. . . . "

"It's there, Cleve. The gold is there. And I need you to help me get it out 'cause you know 'Paches better than any man I know. You're an Apache-fightin' madman and I need you bad. Bad enough to give you an extra five hundred dollars if you stick with me, and your pick of the first whores we find in Tucson."

O'Malley jerked his gaze to Hudson, cocked an eye. "Five hundred?"

"Five hundred. Outta my own pocket."

O'Malley was silent. He looked Hudson over like he was scrutinizing a six-foot pile of shit that had appeared out of the thin desert air.

"That a promise, Page?"

"You're damn tootin' it is, Cleve." Hudson squeezed the big man's arm. "That's how much I need your expert abilities, pard. What do you say?"

O'Malley sighed. "Well," he said, fidgeting again self-importantly, adjusting the heavy load in his arms. "I reckon if you need me that bad. What the hell?"

Hudson smiled and gave O'Malley's shoulder another brotherly squeeze. "Thanks, friend. You won't regret it. I promise you that."

O'Malley spit, adjusted his load, gave a

snort, and started back toward the fire.

Hudson drew on his quirley and watched him go, the oafish sucker. Hudson had no intention of sharing the loot with any of his companions, least of all with O'Malley. When they had gotten the gold out of the desert, O'Malley, Wilks, and Saber would all find themselves in the regrettable position of having .45 slugs in their backs and their shares of the gold in Page Hudson's saddle-bags.

Hudson sucked the quirley, removed it from his lips, and strolled toward the camp, his eyes glazing as he imagined finally getting shut of these three peckerwoods and having all the gold for himself in Mexico.

9

As hard as they rode in the wake of the Indian attack, Cuno and the girl made little headway on the trail of the four killers. They'd lost too much time and the rough country did all it could to obscure the sign.

It was with an air of supreme disgust that, an hour after sundown, Cuno reined his horse off a knoll, bulled through shrubs, and halted Renegade in the gravelly bed of a wash. The girl rode her pinto up beside him.

"We are stopping?"

"What do you think?"

"I think I am hungry."

He sighed as he slipped out of his saddle and began untying his bedroll.

"What are you mad about?" she asked.

"You and your Indians are holding me up. If I hadn't run into you, I might've caught up to Hudson by now."

"Ha!" she exclaimed, angrily dismounting.

"You are mad at yourself because you can't track four horsemen in broad daylight."

Ignoring her, his mind on Hudson, Cuno unsaddled his horse, watered him from his hat, and staked him in a patch of grass on the bank. The girl did likewise. When he'd unrolled his blankets near his saddle, he told the girl to start a small fire, and walked away with his rifle.

"All right, I will tell you," she said, watching him walk away.

He stopped and turned back to her, frowning. "Tell me what?"

"Where Hudson is headed."

Cuno snorted. "Lady, I know where he's headed." He turned away and strode off down the creek bed.

Several hours ago, he'd realized the gang was heading for Krantzburg. Unfamiliar with the country, he'd been slow to remember it was the only town out here. He was letting the girl ride with him because abandoning her would have been the same thing as killing her. As much as she annoyed him, and as much as he wanted her gone, he couldn't kill her.

Adept at night hunting, he shot a rabbit, brought it back to the camp, and roasted it over the fire. The girl ate hungrily with her hands, tearing into the meat like a miner, breaking the bones and sucking out the marrow, then licking the grease off her fingers. When she was through, she wiped her hands on her jeans, took a long pull from her canteen, and curled up on her blankets with a sigh.

Cuno had a smoke, then took up his rifle and, intending to patrol around the camp, began walking away from the fire. Stepping over the girl's legs, he brushed her ankle with his boot. She woke, startled, sitting up and drawing her blanket over her chest defensively.

"I know what you're after," she hissed, her lip curled back. Her eyes reflecting the fire's umber glow were wild, like the impassioned gaze of a threatened wolf bitch. "But you won't get it!"

He squinted down at her, sneering. "You might be able to get a few desperadoes all hot and bothered, but to me you're nothin' but a pain in the ass. Sleep well. You don't have a thing to worry about with me."

With that, he walked away in the darkness. She watched him go, scowling, her lips gradually swelling into a pout.

"Hunh!" she grunted finally, flopping back down and bringing the blanket up to her chin. He might tell himself she had set no blaze in him, but she knew the truth.

★ ★ ★

They were up and riding early the next morning. The girl maintained a haughty silence, and Cuno was grateful. As always, his mind was on Hudson.

At noon, they reined their horses to a halt on the lip of a long, broad valley. Cuno hooked his right boot around his saddle horn and stared down at the little trail town of Krantzburg bustling on the valley floor. Its scattered shops and cabins roughly paralleled a brushy, meandering stream along which trail herds and covered wagons milled.

The town consisted of a hundred-yard main drag lined with wood-frame shops flanked by a few outlying shacks and shanties, and a handful of tents around which wagons sat loaded with whiskey kegs. The smell of new lumber, fresh shit, and bad whiskey wafted on the breeze.

It wasn't a big town, but it was big enough to make picking the four killers out of the boisterous crowd nearly as tricky as following their trail. On the plus side, they'd probably remain here for a day or two, resting and laying in trail supplies.

Lounging in his saddle, Cuno swung his gaze from one side of the settlement to the other, silently promising July that the killers' trail ended here.

"When you find Hudson," the girl said as she too gazed down at the milling burg, "remember he has something that belongs to me."

"I don't care about anything that belongs to you," Cuno muttered, annoyed by her petty concerns and everything else about her, including her looks, which only reminded him of July. "I only care about what belongs to me — and that's those four killers down there."

He felt her agitated gaze on him, and he turned to her with a half-curious, half-amused frown. "Whatever he has, it must be good," he said.

Flushing, she said nothing.

"What is it?"

She only stared down the hill at the town.

"Don't worry," Cuno said after a while, peeling his lips back from his teeth. "I don't give a shit about anything Hudson has, except his life. That's mine." He kneed Renegade and started down the hill.

She watched him for a time, baffled, then kicked the pinto after him.

Descending the hill and curving around a rocky knoll, they entered the town from the east, returning the stares of the Kansas and Nebraska waddies milling on the street. The boardwalks were choked with cattlemen, freighters, and trail supplies waiting to be loaded onto wagons or off-loaded into mercantiles.

Cuno and the girl scoured the crowds for the killers. At the other end of the street they turned around and headed back east at a slow, lumbering walk, weaving around wagons and drays.

"See anything?" he asked the girl, who could pick them out better than he could.

Frustrated, she shook her head.

"I'll check the saloons."

She watched him gig his horse toward a hitching post. "What are you going to do if you find them?"

He wrapped the reins over the post and said as though answering an idiot, "Kill 'em."

"Wait," she urged, staring down at him. "I have an idea — a way to catch them in a trap."

He stared at her, only vaguely curious.

"Hudson," she said, tossing her head and fluffing her hair out, "he likes me. If I could—"

"Forget it."

"What?"

He shook his head once, with ardor. "No traps, no nothing. Just me and them."

"What about my map? If you kill them and

I'm not there, what will happen — ?" She stopped suddenly, muttered a Spanish curse, and cupped her hand to her mouth.

Cuno had turned to the boardwalk. Now he stopped and turned back to her. "Map?"

She only scowled at him, her lip curled back.

His own lips formed a dubious smirk. "A treasure map?"

Eyes burning a hole through him, she said nothing.

Finally, he shrugged. "I find a map on his dead carcass, it's yours."

"You are a crazy gringo if you think I believe you are no more interested in maps than in women," she said, watching him mount the boardwalk and head for a pair of batwings.

He had a beer and watched the crowd. He had a beer in another saloon and watched the crowd there too. He was looking over the crowd in his third saloon, wondering if the gang had split up, when he heard a girl cursing in Spanish-accented English out on the street. Moving to the batwings, he peered outside.

Marcella had been pulled off her horse and was being pawed by two burly freighters. She swung suddenly out of the grasp of the man behind her and gave the one before her a sound thump in the groin with her knee.

"Ahhh!" the man cried, crouching over his jewels, his felt immigrant hat tumbling from his head.

The man behind her shouted, "Why, you — !" as he reached for the knife on his belt.

Cuno had moved onto the boardwalk. He drew his Colt, aimed at the freighter who snarled threats through his red beard.

"Don't do it, friend," Cuno ordered mildly. "Keep that knife in its sheath and live another day."

The man jerked around to face Cuno. His flat features were sunburned and freckled, his red beard stained with tobacco juice. "Who the hell are you?"

"The fella who's gonna send up your ghost if you don't take your hand off that knife."

Several men had gathered to watch; several more were moving down the boardwalk, flanking Cuno. The man Marcella had groined was in the street on his knees, sneering at her as she backed away toward her horse.

The standing freighter did not remove his hand from his knife, and Cuno kept his Colt leveled on him. Finally, the man glanced at his injured friend, as though to throw Cuno off, then whipped back toward Cuno, ripping the knife from its sheath. He'd raised his arm to flick the blade through the air when Cuno's Colt barked.

The freighter stiffened. The dime-sized hole just below his neck looked like a dark blue marble slowly turning red. The blood had begun running down the man's chest when he staggered backward, turned, took three steps as if heading across the street toward the post office, and dropped to his knees.

He remained on his knees for several seconds, facing his friend and rasping, "Kill that bastard . . . for me . . . J.C." Then he fell facedown.

The freighter Marcella had groined looked at Cuno dubiously. When Cuno turned the gun on him, the man shrugged and lifted his hands acquiescently.

"What the hell's happening here, goddamnit?" someone yelled above the pounding of boots on the boardwalk. "Step aside! Step aside!"

A man wearing a town marshal's badge pushed through the crowd. A stocky man with long sideburns, he cuffed his high-crowned hat off his forehead and observed the situation, rolling a toothpick between his lips.

"Did you kill this man?" he asked Cuno.

Cuno holstered his gun but kept his gaze on the freighter kneeling in the street. "He had it comin'."

"The kid's right," said a man behind Cuno. "I saw the whole thing, Marshal. These two were hoorawing the girl, and the kid came to her rescue. Ole McDrummond there pulled a knife." The man smiled. "After the girl kicked the other fella in the oysters."

Someone else whistled. "Man, those nuts must be swellin' up somethin' fierce."

"Hey, J.C.!" another man called. "Your shorts gettin' tight?"

The crowd erupted with laughter.

"All right, shut up!" admonished the marshal. "Everyone move along and let me do my job!"

Grudgingly, the crowd dispersed, leaving Cuno, the girl, the dead man, and his friend, who had pushed himself to his feet. He was short and bald, with a six-inch beard and glassy gray eyes protruding from their sockets. Still wincing with pain, he skewered Marcella with a killing gaze.

Marcella curled her lip and looked away.

The marshal knelt beside the dead freighter and checked for a pulse. "Who are you, kid?" he asked Cuno when he'd made sure the freighter was history.

Cuno told him his name.

"What are you doin' here?"

Cuno glanced at Marcella, who stood by her horse, absently running her hand down the pinto's neck. "Just passin' through," Cuno said.

"Everybody's just passin' through Krantz-burg," the marshal growled, grimly taking Cuno's measure. He looked at Marcella, giving her the up and down with male interest. "And what about you, miss?"

"Me?" she said, her voice acquiring its characteristic edge. "I was doing nothing when these two savages pulled me off my horse. Do you not have laws in this town, or are you too lazy to enforce them?"

The marshal appeared to recoil from the onslaught of Spanish-accented barbs, holding out his hands as though to keep the fiesty girl at bay. "Sorry, miss, I . . ."

"If it hadn't been for this man, who knows where I would be right now. Probably in an alley. On my back!"

"I can't be everywhere at once, you know." Sheepishly, the marshal turned to Cuno. "Well . . . thanks, I reckon . . . for helpin' the girl out."

"I'm still tryin' to decide if she needed it," Cuno said, glancing at Marcella.

The marshal called two passing men off the boardwalk. The men picked up the dead freighter and hauled him off to the undertaker. When the marshal had led the injured freighter off to the jailhouse, Cuno turned to Marcella, who stood with her back to her horse. Chin lowered, she regarded Cuno with a devilish smirk from underneath her brows.

"Maybe you should get a room somewhere," he growled. He started walking toward another saloon, calling over his shoulder, "And stay out of trouble."

"That is the thanks I get for keeping you out of jail?" she snarled behind him. "Men — you are all alike!"

At Miss Kate's Place on a western side street, Page Hudson was doing his second favorite thing behind robbing and killing, taking his pleasure from a whore.

In an upstairs bedroom, he mounted a petite, half-Indian girl named Verna from behind. On the other bed, Kenny Wilks was being ridden by a plump little bird named Ida, who bounced atop him, pressing her hands into his sparrow chest as she worked, sighing and groaning. Kenny grinned up at her, like a boy who'd been given a pellet gun for his birthday. He held his bandaged arm out to the side, so it wouldn't get damaged in the fracas.

Suddenly, the bedroom door opened.

"Hey, what the . . . ?"

Hudson pulled away from the girl and nearly fell off the bed as he grabbed his gun from the holster coiled over a post. He swung the gun toward the open door, but it was Miss Kate standing there — all three hundred pounds of her in a checked yellow dress and bustle riding the wide shelf of her ass. She planted her gnarled fists on her broad hips and pursed her lips disapprovingly.

"Page Hudson," she said, her voice trilling, "there's a man looking for you boys on Main Street!"

Hudson scowled at the woman and let his gun sag in his hand. His heart was still racing from both his workout with the half-breed girl and the unannounced visit from Miss Kate. "You ever heard of knockin', you fat bitch?"

Miss Kate shook her finger at him. "Don't you call me names, Page Hudson, you bottom-feeding, limp-dicked son of a mangy sow bitch in heat! Are you clean, or did you come here with fresh warrants on your head?"

Hudson yelled, "Who the hell's lookin' for me?"

"Some polecat bounty hunter, no doubt. Shing-Su went to the Nations for whiskey and said he heard a man askin' for you with the bartender. If there's law and bounty hunters after you, I don't want you around. If I told you once, I told you a thousand times, I will not have my place torn up by lawmen and bounty hunters! They're worse than outlaws!"

"Shut your fat barn door and get the hell out of here, you cow-assed old nag!"

Her eyes narrowed in their deep, fleshy sockets. "You boys ain't welcome in my place!" she said, shuttling her angry eyes from Hudson to Kenny Wilks, upon whom the blonde still sat, craned around toward the madam. Miss Kate poked a short, crooked finger at the girls. "Ida, Verna — get dressed and come downstairs at once!"

With that, she dug a cheroot stub from her skirt pocket, poked it through the O of her rosebud mouth, and left, leaving the door wide open behind her.

"And shut the fuckin' door!" Hudson yelled, leaping out of bed and slamming the door with a boom.

Naked, his gun still in his hand, he turned to Kenny Wilks. Kenny was still on the bed, propped on his elbows and eyeing Hudson curiously. Both girls had climbed out of bed and were gathering their clothes, which Hudson and Wilks had practically torn off their backs in a lustful frenzy.

Hudson was about to speak, then something caught his eye. "Jesus Christ, Kenny — you're hung like a horse!"

Kenny looked down and nodded. "It runs in the family. You shoulda seen my grandfather." He and Hudson stared silently at his pecker. Then Wilks's expression turned curious again. "Who do you suppose is asking for us uptown?"

Hudson tore his gaze from Wilks's sausage, shook his head, and looked around for his jeans. "I don't know, but we best get Clevis and Billy and check it out. Whoever it is, I wanna find *him* before he finds *us*."

10

At ten o'clock that night, Cuno stood at the bar in the Trailside Saloon and Dance Hall, slowly sipping his third beer of the evening while keeping an eye on the batwings for the appearance of Hudson's crew.

From what he remembered and from Marcella's descriptions, he thought he'd recognize all of them, though he'd only seen Hudson and Wilks. Saber shouldn't be too hard to pick out of a crowd. Marcella said he'd been named appropriately; he was tall, lean, hawk-nosed, and always wore a gray Confederate forage cap. O'Malley was big and shaggy, with a face like a Halloween pumpkin.

Around Cuno, the crowd milled under a heavy cloud of tobacco smoke while a gray-haired gent in a frayed frock coat and opera hat banged on a piano. Several waddies and pleasure girls danced, laughing and carrying on, often tripping over each other's feet. A girl in a short, pink dress broke a heel and fell on her ass, and the crowd erupted in applause.

Cuno turned away, his expression stony. He sipped his beer.

Where were they? Surely, if they were in town, they'd make the saloon rounds this evening. And they had to be in town. If they were headed into the rough country south of here, they'd need fresh horses and trail supplies.

"Hi there, fella," said a woman's voice to his right.

He turned to see a short, dark-haired girl move toward him through the crowd of men eyeing her admiringly. She smiled at Cuno. His chest tightened. This girl, like Marcella, looked a little like July in the lips and around the eyes. But then, most every girl reminded him of the one he had loved and had lost.

She stopped before him, gave her hip a coquettish bounce, and canted her head to one side, smiling smokily. "My name's Rose."

He took a long drink from his beer and looked away. Her smile faded, and the girl walked on.

Cuno finished the beer and ordered another. He'd spent time in Krantzburg's four saloons, and he'd had too much to drink for accurate shooting, if the night came to that, but he suddenly didn't care. He drank a third of his next beer, standing with his back to the bar, jostled by the crowd around him, lost in the din but keeping an eye peeled on the batwings.

As his eyes swept the room again, they caught on a familiar face turned toward him. It was the freighter Marcella had groined earlier. He was seated at a table about twenty feet out on the floor. His hat was tipped back on his head, and a long cheroot sagged from his lips. His drink-bleary, bulbous eyes penetrated Cuno with a savage stare.

Cuno looked away, showing no interest. When he looked back, the man was still staring at him, and the other five men around the table were too. The freighter chewed his cigar and said something to the others without removing his gaze from Cuno.

Wanting no trouble with the freighter, Cuno took another sip from his beer and set it on the bar. He'd head to one of the other saloons for a while, return here in a couple of hours, when the freighter had had his fill of liquor and cards and had moved on.

With that intention, not caring if his retreat appeared cowardly, he turned and shoved his way toward the door, walking slowly but keeping his head turned enough that he could detect any fast movement behind him.

He was two steps from the batwings when chair legs were raked across the floor with a squeaky bark. His back prickled as, in the corner of his right eye, he saw the freighter jump to his feet. Cuno wheeled, unsnapping his trigger thong.

"You coward!" the freighter cried in a whiskey-thick voice, jutting an accusing arm at Cuno. "Get back here and face me like a man. You killed my partner, you son of a bitch!"

The man's voice roared above the din, silencing it. The piano clattered to a stop. All faces turned to the drunk freighter and then to Cuno. Nervously, the crowd parted between them.

Cuno returned the man's stare, saying nothing, hands hanging at his sides.

"You killed Mack!" the freighter cried. He turned to one of the men who had been sitting at the table but who had scrambled away and was now standing off to the side, still holding his cards. "You seen it, didn't you, Earl?"

Earl glared at Cuno. "I seen it."

The freighter returned his infuriated gaze to Cuno. "Well, say somethin' for yourself, goddamnit!"

Cuno moved his lips tightly. "I reckon you said it all, friend. All I can add is, if you touch that hogleg on your hip, you're gonna die tonight." His voice was hard, even, barely above a whisper.

The freighter studied him up and down, squinting. Doubt flickered in his eyes. Then he spit the cheroot from his lips and stepped back from the table, holding his hands out from his hips. "You think you're pretty fast, eh?"

Cuno stared at him.

"All you younkers think you're fast. You read too many stories. But all you're really fast for is the grave."

Earl cleared his throat. "I don't know, J.C. I seen him today, and he looked pretty durn fast to me."

Earl's warning evoked another flicker of doubt in the freighter's eyes. It was unnerving the way Cuno stared at him, saying nothing. Without moving his head, his gaze swept the room. Men and pleasure girls watched expectantly, smoke curling from their cigars and cigarettes, drinks clenched in their fists.

The freighter could not back down. Not now, after he'd called Cuno's number. Cuno saw the grim resolve in the man's eyes.

A second later it was over. A single shot from Cuno's Colt slammed into J.C.'s chest before the freighter had gotten the barrel free of his toed holster. The man was nearly blown off his feet, falling backward onto a table, tipping it over and scattering bottles, glasses, and playing cards. Several seconds passed before a girl screamed.

Cuno cursed and holstered his smoking gun. When the marshal appeared several minutes later, having been summoned by one of the bartenders, Cuno was waiting for him by the bar, his back to the mahogany, a grim cast to his features.

The marshal and a tall, dark-haired deputy wielding a shotgun checked the freighter. Then, while the deputy and two other men hauled the freighter out the back, the marshal strode stiffly over to Cuno and stared up at him, thumbs tucked into the cartridge belt nearly hidden by his bulging belly.

"I don't need to hear what happened. I can guess. He was tryin' to get even for his partner."

"That's right."

"Well, that's your bad luck. I want you out of town tomorrow morning before full light. Understand?"

Cuno frowned, anger burning under his collar. "He gave me no choice."

"Sorry, kid. I've had my fill," the marshal said, shaking his head. Holding out his hand, he added, "I'll take your hogleg butt-first. You can pick it up tomorrow on your way out of town."

Cuno was incredulous. "You can't take my gun. What if — ?"

"What if what — you get in trouble again? Guess you'll have to try somethin' new, like talkin' your way out of it. Hand it over . . . or spend the night in the lockup."

Cuno stared at the thickly built lawman, who gazed up at Cuno, hand extended. Finally, Cuno palmed his Colt and set it in the marshal's open hand.

The marshal stuck the gun behind his cartridge belt. "You're outta here tomorrow. Before nine. If I see you after that, I'm gonna turn the key on you." He turned, talked to the bartender for a few minutes, then gave Cuno a hard look as he left.

Cuno stepped through the batwings and into the night, cursing Marcella Jiminez. He knew his having to kill two men in the past few hours wasn't directly her fault, but without her here, it wouldn't have happened. Now he would have to hide out from the marshal while scouring Krantzburg for the Hudson gang. Despite the marshal's warning, he intended to go nowhere until he'd either found the gang or had given up hope of finding them here.

Somehow, he'd find them. If not here, then elsewhere. He would never give up.

Feeling naked without his .45, he turned left and walked up the street, toward the livery barn where he'd stabled his horse. In his saddlebags was a spare Colt; he had no intention of searching for Hudson's gang unarmed.

He'd taken ten steps before two people walked out of an alley, stepping onto the boardwalk and strolling toward him. They were a man and a woman, walking arm in arm. The man staggered as though drunk and nearly fell as, laughing, he turned to nuzzle the woman's neck. Cuno was about to pass them when he stopped suddenly, gazing down at Marcella Jiminez.

She looked up at him as the tall man nuzzled her cheek. "What?" she asked Cuno, annoyance flashing in her eyes beneath her hat. "I must survive, no? Now that you let Page Hudson get away. What would you have me do, sling hash for pennies?"

The man lifted his head, which lolled drunkenly on his shoulders, and squinted his bleary eyes at Cuno. "Yeah," he said, his voice sounding like his tongue was stuck to the roof of his mouth. "Want her slingin' hash?" He grinned down at Marcella, cupping one of her breasts through her blouse.

"A girl that looks like this?"

"Come on!" Marcella ordered her customer, yanking his arm, pushing and pulling him up the boardwalk.

Cuno turned to watch them amble off in the darkness, Marcella leading the way. They paused near the Trailside Saloon, and Marcella guided the stumbling cowboy up an outside stairway. Apparently, she'd worked out a deal with the saloon's owner whereby she could use one of his upstairs rooms for a cut of her profits.

Cuno rubbed his jaw as she and the cowboy disappeared in the darkness, the man chuckling and softly singing. Then Cuno turned and resumed his walk toward the livery barn.

He was crossing the street at an angle when he heard the boardwalk squeak behind him. Wheeling, he touched his holster, forgetting the gun wasn't there. Peering at the line of stores silhouetted against the starry sky, he saw no one suspicious, only a few drovers in Texas hats and chaps milling around the hitch racks farther down the street where the saloons were still hopping. This end of the street was dark and quiet.

Far off in the buttes, a coyote yapped.

Feeling naked without his gun, Cuno continued on toward the livery barn standing alone across the street, its peaked roof blocking the stars. He was about to pull one of the two big doors open when he heard a sharp intake of air behind him. A boot kicked a stone. Before Cuno could turn, someone hit him a glancing blow on the back of his head.

Stunned, he dropped to his knees.

"Grab him!" someone yelled with hushed vehemence.

Page Hudson shoved the three-foot length of leaded rawhide behind his pistol belt, and grabbed Cuno's right arm while Clevis O'Malley grabbed his left. They dragged Cuno's sagging bulk around to the side of the livery barn, into the dense shadows under the overhanging roof.

Kenny Wilks and Billy Saber ran up behind them.

"Is it him? Is it Massey?" Saber asked, breathlessly eager.

"It's him, all right," Hudson growled, giving Cuno a hard kick in the ribs. Cuno grunted and grabbed his stomach. "I got a good look at him in the saloon window, after he shot some freighter."

Hudson glared down at the young man, who cursed as he shook his head from side to side, trying to clear the cobwebs. Hudson had hit him a pretty good blow with the quirt.

"Well, we gonna kill him, or what?" O'Malley asked, raising his revolver.

Hudson grabbed O'Malley's wrist, sending wary glances up and down the street. "In the riverbed out back." He grabbed Massey's right arm and pulled. "Come on, Cleve. Grab him, let's go!"

Swimming up through the brain fog and summoning all his strength, Cuno heaved his arm free of Hudson's grip. Shoving himself up against the barn, he thrust the toe of his right boot into O'Malley's thigh. As the Irishman squealed and bent forward, cursing, Cuno turned left, whipping his arm out. He'd intended to hit the slight, bowler-hatted man standing there in the face, but Cuno's right knee buckled, and his fist connected instead with Wilks's left arm. Wilks grabbed the arm, howling and sidle-hopping into the shadows.

Cuno was trying to push off his right knee when Hudson punched his jaw. A gun exploded, and Cuno felt the slug brush his left ear as he hit the dirt, his head swirling and teeth gnashing against the pain.

"Goddamnit, Billy — I said no shootin'!"

"What the hell was I s'posed to do?"

Another voice wailed, "The sumbitch opened my arm up! Ohhh!"

Suddenly, gunfire erupted from the street.

It sounded like a small-caliber pistol. Cuno rolled onto his chest and covered his head, hearing Hudson's men curse and yell as the slugs plunked the ground and tore into the livery barn, setting the stock inside to bellowing and kicking their stalls.

"Outta here — get outta here!" one of the men yelled.

There was one more shot, and then only the sound of footfalls retreating behind the barn.

Cuno lowered his arms and lifted his chin. A slender, jean-clad figure ran toward him. The curves belonged to a woman. Long, dark hair bounced on her shoulders, beneath a man's felt hat, its acorn fastener swaying beneath her chin.

Marcella Jiminez knelt beside Cuno. Her .36 Smith & Wesson smoked in her slender hand. Her voice was high with ardor. "Was it him? Was it Hudson?"

Cuno tried to speak, but his voice caught in his throat, the nearly unendurable pain in his head thumbing it back down his windpipe. In spite of the pain, he nodded and tried to rise. It was no use; his strength was gone, replaced by a head-spinning, heavy-limbed nausea.

"It was him!" Marcella cried with angry zeal and frustration.

She bounded to her feet and ran down the side of the barn, yelling in Spanish as she looked around for evidence she'd done any damage with her .36. She saw nothing, not even a blood splatter.

"They got away!" she cried. "They got *away!*"

She clapped her hands to her face, cuffing her hat off her head, letting it hang down her back from its thong. She stumbled back to Cuno and knelt down. "Damnit, do you know where they are going?" she cried, jerking his shoulder. "Do you know where they are going?"

Cuno winced and pushed himself up on his arms and legs. "Now, how in the hell would I know where they're going?" he rasped, squeezing his eyes closed against the flares going off behind his lids. Fatigue and fury hammered his head, right along with the pain. Beneath it, however, was the satisfaction of knowing Hudson's gang was in town.

"Mierda!" she raged, whipping her head around to look down the side of the barn where all four men had disappeared.

She wanted to run after them, but she had no more shells for her pistol. The rest were in her room.

A few minutes ago, from the top of the

saloon's outside stairs, she'd seen two men pass on the boardwalk behind Cuno, as if following him. The darkness hid their features, but she had her suspicions. Abandoning her befuddled customer, Marcella had retrieved her pistol from her room, in her haste forgetting to grab spare shells, and descended the outside stairs at a run. Clinging to the railing as though to the railing of a sinking ship, the drunken cowboy had stared after her in slack-jawed awe.

Not only was she out of ammunition, she reflected now, but she was only one woman against four men — four seasoned killers. She could not go after all four alone.

"Mierda!" she cried again from the depths of her deep frustration.

"Hey, what the hell's going on over there?"

She and Cuno turned to the street. Two shadows — one short and stocky, the other tall and broadly built — were heading this way from the other side of the street. The tall man carried a shotgun. The short man, a pistol. Badges flashed on their vests.

"Ah, shit," Cuno said, pressing his fists to his temples.

11

Marcella Jiminez had ridden on the wrong side of the law enough times that when she saw the two lawmen running toward her, her first and last impulse was to run. To hell with Cuno Massey.

That was another of her primary impulses — to worry about herself first. If she had any worry left over, she could spread it around. But she rarely had any left over.

She knew she hadn't done anything wrong tonight. In fact, she'd saved a man's life. But she did not wish to spend several hours in a jailhouse, answering foolish questions posed by gringo lawmen who would probably hold her longer than necessary just to stare at her tits or try to rape her in one of their cells.

Bounding to her feet, not taking so much as a second glance at Cuno, she ran down the dark corridor between the livery barn and the feed store. Her low-heeled boots skidding as she slowed for the turn at the rear of the feed store, she took a hard right and disappeared.

"Stop!" the marshal shouted as he and the deputy approached Cuno, who was sitting, bent legs spread, on his butt. "Johnny, get after her, goddamnit!"

As the marshal stopped before Cuno, his deputy disappeared down the corridor, grunting, boots squeaking, his holster slapping his thigh. Cuno looked up at the marshal. The marshal looked down at Cuno.

"I hate to keep singin' the same hymn, but it wasn't my fault." Cuno rolled his shoulders and waited for the clouds to clear.

His head ached like hell, but he didn't feel so bad. Hudson was here in Krantzburg.

"And I hate to beat the same drum," the marshal said, his voice raised and his brows furrowed, "but what in the hell kinda trouble you get yourself into now, and who in the hell was the girl with the six-shooter?"

Cuno probed the back of his head with his left hand, where Hudson had nailed him with the leaded quirt. He looked at his blood-smeared fingers and said, "I reckon some cowpokes came up a little short at the faro tables and decided to turn me inside out."

"That the same girl you was with earlier?"

Cuno shrugged. "I didn't get a good look

149

at her." He didn't want to explain the real nature of the trouble to the marshal. Hudson and his gang were all his and only his.

"Is that right?" the marshal said, staring at Cuno skeptically. "Troublemakin' women just happen to follow you around, that it?"

"I reckon."

The sheriff spit angrily. "How many of these here 'cowpokes' were there?"

Cuno shrugged. "Didn't have time to count."

Just then, footsteps sounded back along the barn. It was the deputy walking toward them, kicking a can, breathing hard.

"No luck, Marshal," the big man said as he approached, holding his shotgun barrel-up. "That girl lit out like a mule with its tail on fire." He frowned down at Cuno. "Say, isn't he the fella that shot that freighter?"

"That's him. Massey, wasn't it?"

Cuno didn't say anything. In spite of his aching head, he was thinking about Hudson. He had a bull by the tail and would not let go.

"Who's the girl?" the deputy asked.

Straightening, his legs creaking audibly, the marshal said skeptically as he stared down at Cuno, "He claims men rolled him, and the girl saved his hide. But he doesn't know who she was."

The deputy laughed. "Well, she sure slung the lead. Doesn't look like she hit anything, though." He chuckled again as he mopped his brow with a red handkerchief with white polka dots. "Why do you s'pose she run off so fast?"

"Yeah, why do you s'pose?" the marshal mused aloud, scratching his head and glaring at Cuno.

Cuno shrugged again and eased himself to his feet. His head still grieved him terribly, but the world was not spinning quite as fast as before. He'd retrieve his gun from his saddlebags and see what he could still do tonight about Hudson. "Well, I reckon I'll be—"

"You're not going anywhere," the marshal said, shuffling back a step and drawing his revolver. He ratcheted back the hammer. "Except to the skookum house."

Cuno turned to him, his voice low but sharp. "You can't lock me up, Marshal. I was the one who was rolled. Thanks to you, I'm not even armed."

"You might've been rolled, all right," the marshal allowed. "But you're gonna spend the night in the lockup just the same. Give me time to stick a fork in your story and go over my wanted dodgers. And give you time to refresh your memory about the girl."

Cuno stared at the lawman, nostrils flaring.

"I'm thinkin' he might be part of a bigger gang in town," the marshal said, turning to the deputy with a cunning grimace. "A bigger gang maybe at war with itself." He looked at Cuno again. "Until I can go through my wanted dodgers, consider yourself a guest of the city of Krantzburg." He jabbed his gun into Cuno's ribs. "Move!"

Cuno turned to the deputy. The big man lowered his shotgun at Cuno's belly, stuck his finger through the trigger guard, and smiled grimly through his mustache.

Cuno hesitated. Hudson was here in Krantzburg, but for how long? Cuno needed to get after him. Now. Tonight.

He stared at the double-bore shotgun yawning at his middle. The deputy must have read his mind. He said, "Go ahead, amigo. Try it. Save me swampin' out your cell and fetchin' your breakfast in the mornin'."

A tense silence yawned. Cuno stared into the deputy's young but determined eyes. He shuttled his gaze to the marshal, who gazed back at him, his own Remington aimed at Cuno's side, a thin smile on his red-mottled, pear-shaped face.

A nerve twitched in Cuno's jaw. He

couldn't avenge July's murder if he was dead. Sighing with resignation, he turned and started walking slowly along the street. The movement caused the hammer in his head to resume its pounding. His feet felt like lead.

"Thought you'd see it my way," the marshal said, falling in behind him.

Hudson, O'Malley, Saber, and Wilks rounded the corner near the blacksmith shop and approached their horses tied to the hitching post. Wilks held his bloody arm, grunting and sighing with pain.

"Let's head back to Miss Kate's place," Hudson said, grabbing his reins off the rack. "We've been safe there so far. Tomorrow we'll lay in trail supplies and head south."

"What about Massey?" Clevis O'Malley asked, his voice deep with menace. Massey had given his thigh a good shot with his boot, and O'Malley had limped all the way there, feeling like he'd been shot with a big-caliber rifle. The kid would pay for that. O'Malley ground his teeth. He'd pay well.

None of them knew they'd been driven away from Massey by a young woman, least of all a young woman named Marcella Jiminez. None had gotten a look at the shooter in the dark. They knew only that they'd been shot at and that several bullets had come close. In fact, Hudson himself sported a frayed hole in his hat crown.

He toed a stirrup and swung up on his horse. "He's followed us this far; he'll keep followin' us. We'll settle with him and the son of a bitch he's ridin' with down south somewhere."

"What about my arm?" Kenny Wilks moaned. "It's opened up again. I'm about to bleed dry!"

"Shut the hell up and quit worryin' about your arm, Kenny," Hudson said, his mount fiddle-footing in half circles. "That big third leg is wasted on you — you freakin' Nancy-boy! *Wasted!*"

They cantered their horses through the back streets of Krantzburg. There were several windows dimly lit at Miss Kate's place, which was an old stage depot of age-blackened logs, to which Kate had added a clapoard second story, near a creek at the edge of town. As the men slowed their horses in the yard, Hudson turned to the other three, pressing a finger to his lips.

"Quietly, boys. Quietly. Miss Kate's feathers are a little ruffled this evenin'."

They stabled their horses in the barn, then crossed the yard to the house. Hudson opened the door slowly, quietly peering into

154

the small parlor to his right. Several scantily clad girls were lounging around the shabby sofas and fainting couches with half-dressed men. The cheap whiskey was flowing freely.

The conversations died, and dull-eyed faces turned to Hudson's gang. Several of the men in the room frowned warily. Several girls paled. Hudson didn't think too much about it. Earlier in the night he'd beaten a mule skinner senseless for using a wrist slide during a card game, and he supposed the girls were still a little edgy. And, of course, Miss Kate had barred him and the boys from the premises. Not seeing the old bitch around, however, Hudson swaggered into the room, the other three men following close on his heels.

"Where's Kate?" Hudson asked one of the girls.

The girl stared at him for a few seconds, then said dully, "Out . . . with a gentleman caller."

"Good," Hudson said. "Where's Patty?"

No one said anything.

"Where in the hell's Patty?" Hudson asked again, growing hot.

"In the kitchen," one of the girls said, nodding to indicate the Z-frame door off the dining room, which was only one long table abutted with benches and on which several empty bottles sat amidst overflowing ash trays. A black cat had one of the bottles over on its side and was running its tongue along the rim.

"For chrissakes," Hudson grumbled impatiently as he wheeled and pushed through the kitchen door.

The slight girl in a pale green wrapper, blond hair coiled atop her head, was chunking wood in the iron range. "Page!" she exclaimed, looking surprised. "What are you doin' back here?"

Hudson chuckled, grabbed the girl's wrist, and pulled her toward the door. "Come on, let's go upstairs. I got some thinkin' to do, and you know how I do my best thinkin'."

"I-I can't, Page. I gotta heat water for baths!"

"Later." He jerked her through a door and up a narrow stairs. Her slippered feet did a muffled, staccato patter on the squeaky board steps. Page took them three at a time, barely making any noise at all.

At the top was a narrow, unlit hall. Behind a closed door, a girl sang an Irish ballad out of tune. Behind another, O'Malley chuckled as another girl was apparently taking the big man's mind off his bruised thigh. One door was open. Page pulled the girl through it, kicked off his boots, and began taking off his clothes.

"Page, please," the girl whined. She looked at him, her lips trembling.

"Don't worry about Kate," Hudson said, thoroughly befuddled. "She gives me any trouble, I'll shove my pistol up her fat ass and pull the trigger."

"It's not Miss Kate, it's—"

"Stop flappin' your lips, Patty flower, and get your clothes off. Let's get to work."

She did, and they did. But Patty's heart wasn't in it. She worked atop Hudson stiffly, bouncing on her knees. Her face was pale and expressionless, and fine lines etched the skin above the bridge of her nose. Her little nipples between his index fingers and thumbs were soft as fresh raisins.

Hudson grabbed her hips and bounced her up and down. He was frustrated. "Jesus Christ, girl. Can't you work up a little enthusiasm? Shit, an hour ago—"

"Shhh!"

Hudson looked up at her, frowning. The stairs squeaked, as though someone were walking up them on the balls of his feet.

"What's the matter?" Hudson asked the girl.

"Oh, God!" she said thinly.

"What the hell is it?"

She clapped her hands over his mouth and turned her head, listening. Slow, muffled footfalls came from the hall.

"It's him!" the girl whispered.

Page raked her hands from his mouth. "Who?"

"There was a man," she said, her voice quaking, cheeks bleached with fear. "He came earlier. A lawman. He was lookin' for you. He said he knew you'd been here and if you came again, we were supposed to find him and tell him. If we didn't, he'd arrest us all, shoot the cats, and burn the house down!"

"Shit!"

"Please don't let me die, Page!"

Rising, Hudson flung the girl away. She hit the floor with a scream. Naked, his dirty-blond hair flying around his shoulders, Hudson grabbed the Colt from the holster coiled over a chair back.

He'd just started turning toward the door when the door exploded inward, wood shards flying from the latch. A medium-tall man in a dark tunic and red neckerchief bounded into the room, a heavy silver pistol extended toward the bed. An oval badge glinted on his chest. He wore a droopy mustache and goatee, and his hat cord swung beneath his chin.

Page fired first. The man yelled, showing his teeth, and stumbled back against the wall. "Greet the devil for me, Ranger!" Page cried, triggering another shot.

The man dodged the bullet, hitting the floor, rolling off a shoulder, and coming up firing. He was moving too quickly for accurate shooting, however. Crouched behind a bedpost, Page triggered three more fast rounds. Wailing, the lawman stumbled back, blood sprouting from the slugs tearing gouts of flesh and bone from his cheeks. His pistol leapt from his hands to clatter to the floor near the girl, who crouched on her hands and knees, arms around her head, screaming.

Hudson fired another round into the lawman's red neckerchief blousing up from his chest. The man plunged backward through the window behind him, glass exploding. There was a clamorous, house-shaking thump as he hit the porch roof, a baleful cry, and then nothing but the girl's terrified screams.

"Shut up!" Page shouted, and she did, lowering her head to the floor and sobbing into the rug.

Wheeling, Page bolted into the hall, gun extended. His three partners were there, half-dressed, pistols in their hands. Wilks had a fresh bandage on his arm, but still looked drawn. O'Malley wore only his cowboy hat, his free hand cupped over his privates.

"What in the name of Sam Houston . . . ?"

"A Ranger," Page said, his heart hammering, his breath coming in short, ragged gasps. "Don't ask me where he came from, but that was a fucking Ranger."

"Shit!" Kenny Wilks exclaimed. "I need one good night's rest or my arm's gonna rot *off!*"

Billy Saber ran into Hudson's room and yelled from the window, "I don't see anyone else in the yard, and the horses look quiet."

"Get dressed, boys," Hudson said, turning back into his room, tossing his empty gun on the bed, and grabbing his jeans off the floor. "We're pullin' out!"

12

The next morning, Cuno Massey woke with a start. He thought he'd heard July screaming. Opening his eyes and seeing the thick ceiling logs and barred window through which bright morning light slanted, he remembered with a pang of consternation that the tin stars had thrown him in jail.

His head thudded sharply and then relented a little.

Maybe his marbles were settling.

He pushed himself up and swung his feet to the floor, lowered his head to his hands. The movement had reawakened the throbbing steam engine in his head. When he looked up, he saw a tray on the rough wooden table. On the tray sat a tin mug of coffee, a bowl of lumpy oatmeal, and a plate of buttered toast. Cuno wasn't hungry, but he reached for the toast anyway. Cold. He sipped the tepid coffee.

Looking around, he saw that two other men occupied the cell block. One was a tall, bald, black man, curled on his cot. Another was a wizened old man with a white beard he combed with both hands while sitting on the edge of his cot, staring at the floor.

Cuno took another bite of the toast for sustenance, and drank the coffee. It made him feel a little better. The only thing that would make him feel anywhere near well, however, was getting out of this jail cell and getting back after Page Hudson. The sole good that had come from last night was knowing that Hudson's gang was in town. But they wouldn't be in town long.

Cuno rapped his empty cup against the bars. "Hey, Marshal!" he yelled at the cell block door to his right. "Time to let me outta here!"

The man had no legal right to hold him. Cuno hadn't done anything wrong. But he also knew that small-town lawmen did not always pay heed to legal rights. But the marshal had had time to check his wanted dodgers and see that Cuno wasn't wanted — by the law anyway.

Lifting his head from his pillow, the black man cried, "Be still, will ye? I'm tryin' to sleep!"

Cuno waited, listening. Finally, a key rat-

162

tled in the cell block door. The door opened and a slight young man, maybe thirteen or fourteen, appeared. He had freckles and a close-fitting cap of curly red hair.

"What's the problem in here?" the kid called, trying to sound tough.

"Where's the marshal?" Cuno asked.

"Busy. There was a shootin' in town last night. An Arizona Ranger was killed. He and Johnny are out with a posse."

Cuno's face flushed with fury. "So what's he gonna do — leave me here to rot? I have to get outta here!"

The kid scrunched up his thin lips and squinted one eye. It made him look more comical than nasty. "You'll just have to wait. And don't give me no trouble, 'cause trouble's my middle name."

With a punctuating nod, the kid ducked back into the main office, drawing the door closed behind him. The black man cackled, glanced at Cuno humorously, then lowered his bald head again to his pillow.

"That's Jug," he said. "Marshal's nephew. The jailer." He chuckled again.

Cuno paced in the cell for most of the day, pausing only to roll a smoke or stare in frustration out the barred window, at the grassy lot behind the jail where an occasional brindle dog passed and where trash and tumbleweeds blew. Hudson and his men probably never thought about the young woman they'd killed, much less had any regrets about killing her. The realization made Cuno's jaws ache with rage.

Once, two boys crossed the lot wielding bows and arrows whittled from willow sticks. One of the boys shot an arrow through the bars, hitting Cuno in the back as he paced.

More frustrated at the wait for the marshal than at the boys, Cuno picked up the arrow, snapped it between his fingers, and thrust it back out the window.

The black man clapped his hands and wheezed with laughter. The bearded oldster still sat on his cot, staring at the floor and mumbling, "I need a drink *bad* . . . I need a drink *bad* . . . *!*"

Around three, a thunderstorm rolled in, filling the lot with an eerie, green-purple light and cloaking it with pale, slanting rain. The marshal appeared a half hour later, soaked to the bone and looking frustrated. He wore a yellow rain slicker and, to Cuno's relief, had a ring of keys in his hand.

"'Bout time," Cuno groused, donning his hat when the marshal had released the other two men and was making his way to Cuno's cell.

"Sounds to me like you wanna have another night on the town," the marshal said, pausing with the key before the lock. His eyes were threatening. "That be a pity too since I didn't see your face on any o' my wanted dodgers. I could always hold you till the new batch came in, though."

Cuno dropped his eyes, trying to look diffident. "Sorry."

"That's more like it."

The marshal opened the door. He wasn't wearing his hat, and his thin, dark-brown hair lay in wet swirls against his scalp.

"Who were you chasing?" Cuno asked him. He'd been wondering if it could have been Hudson.

"Four hard cases killed a Ranger last night. The man must've recognized the gang in one of the saloons and followed them over to a brothel. The fool should've waited for help. Instead, he's pushin' up ocotillo on boot hill."

The marshal gave a snort. "My deputy and the Ranger's partner are still out with a small posse. The rest of us turned back on account of the rain." He impaled Cuno with a hard scrutiny. "Say, I wonder if they're the same men that jumped you last night. . . ."

Cuno shrugged, his face revealing nothing. *The bastards had left town.* . . . "Beats the hell out of me."

The marshal rubbed his chin thoughtfully, squinting his pale, weary eyes. "Their leader's a maggot named Hudson. Ever hear of him?"

Cuno froze, one hand on the open cell door. "Hudson?"

"That's right," the marshal said. "Sound familiar?"

Cuno shook his head. "Never heard of him, Marshal."

The marshal kept staring at Cuno as raindrops slid down his face and neck. He obviously had his suspicions, but he was too tired to pursue them.

Finally, he turned, grumbling, and headed for the open cell block door. Cuno followed him, barely containing his urgent need to run, to get after Hudson.

In the front office, the marshal produced Cuno's Colt and gun belt from a drawer in his battered rolltop. "Now get outta town and don't come back," he ordered, shrugging out of his slicker with an angry snarl.

Cuno wrapped the belt around his waist and cinched it, then set his hat gingerly on his head, which still ached but with less vigor than earlier.

"Intend to do just that, Marshal," he said as he opened the door.

He stopped in the open doorway and

gazed across the street. He didn't see much. His thoughts were with Hudson. After a moment, he turned back to the marshal, conjuring another nonchalant expression while ignoring the fervent ringing the news of Hudson had brought to his ears.

"Say, which way were those shooters headed anyway, Marshal?"

His back to Cuno, the lawman was crouched over a cabinet, filling a dented percolator with coffee from a tin can. He swung his head around, scowling. "Huh?"

"Which way did you say those shooters were headed?" Cuno smiled affably. "Maybe I'll ride the other way. Sure don't want any more trouble."

The marshal squinted at him skeptically, holding a heaping spoon before the coffee can. "South, if it's any of your business."

"Well, then, maybe I'll head north." Cuno tipped his hat to the lawman and went out, closing the door behind him.

He stood on the hard patch of sunken ground under the awning, watching the rain pelt the mud puddles up and down the street and slick the backs of horses hunched at tie rails. The mercantile reared directly across the street. Several freighters stood around on the loading dock, smoking under the awning and chatting while sending occasional glances skyward. The clouds appeared to be lifting, and the gunmetal color was running toward gray, with faded yellow splotches around the edges.

Hudson was on the run, heading south. But this rain would obliterate his tracks. Not even an Apache could track him after a gully-washer like this one.

The knowledge was a sharp-edged pit in Cuno's belly.

He stood there thinking for several minutes. Finally, an idea occurred to him. He winced at it, repelled by it, because it involved the girl. He wanted nothing more to do with the obstinate Mexican, but he could think of no other way.

Finally, grumbling, he tipped his hat over his eyes and trotted across the street, hunching his shoulders against the deluge. He followed the boardwalk to the Trailside Saloon.

Due to the rain, there was an unusually boisterous crowd milling inside for this time of the day. The din was constant, and cigarette smoke hung heavy beneath the rafters, fighting the fresh smell of the rain wafting through the batwings.

Cuno looked around, scanning the room with narrowed eyes. Not finding who he was looking for, he pushed his way to the back of the room, where a rosy-cheeked man played a fiddle drowned out by the din, and climbed the stairs.

On the second story, six or seven doors faced each side of the long, narrow hall. Cuno was moving down the shabbily carpeted corridor, listening at the doors, when one opened a few feet ahead on the right. A short, burly man with a carefully trimmed beard, bowler hat, and round, wire-framed spectacles stepped out, flushed and glassy-eyed. Seeing Cuno, he grinned around the freshly lit stogie in his mouth.

"If you're lookin' for the Mex," he said as he passed, "you're in for a treat!"

Cuno opened the door the man had just closed, and stepped inside. It was a small room with a single, grimy window and a lumpy, brass-framed bed. Marcella sat on the edge of the bed, her feet on the floor, her slender, naked back facing Cuno behind the dark curtain of her hair.

She was lighting a cigarette, blowing smoke and waving out the match.

Turning her head to one side but not really looking at him, revealing the small, purple birthmark on her neck, she said with a bored, tired air, "*Hola, amigo.* Make yourself comfortable, and I will be with you after my cigarette."

Cuno stood stiffly just inside the door,

which he hadn't bothered to close. He noted only half-consciously that she looked lovely naked — small and fragile, with vanilla skin and heavy breasts. Her back couldn't have been much wider than his two hands placed side by side, halved by her delicate, curving spine.

"Where's Hudson headed?" he asked in a tight, grim voice barely containing his ardor.

Surprised, she whipped her head around. Seeing him, she wrinkled her nose and turned back to the wall. "Is it the *man tracker* who needed a woman to save his life?"

Ignoring the comment, he asked again, "Where's Hudson headed?"

"Why don't you track him?" she asked reasonably. "You are such a good tracker."

He walked stiffly around the bed, clamped his left hand around her neck, slammed her back on the rumpled sheets, and drew his Colt. He pressed the barrel to her forehead and thumbed back the hammer.

She stared up at him fearlessly, her brown eyes glazed with gray light from the window.

"Go ahead," she taunted. "Pull the trigger of your big gun."

He squeezed her neck. "You don't think I will?"

"No, I don't," she spit with defiance. To

his exasperation, she smiled. "Do you think I would care if you did? What do I have to lose?" She moved her head slightly, sliding her eyes over the fly-specked plaster walls, the cluttered dresser with its cracked mirror and chipped water pitcher and bowl. In the bowl were coins — tips from satisfied customers, no doubt — and cigarette butts. Her clothes lay in a rumpled pile in a corner.

"All my life I have been either an outlaw's woman or a whore," she said. "I have never had a real life or been a real person anyone cared about, except to lay between my legs." Her brown eyes had grown nearly black, the even blacker pupils contracting and expanding. "Why would I fear death?"

Still pressing the gun to her head, he stared down at her. She stared impassively back at him, her eyes slightly narrowed around the barrel. It was an off-putting stare, and it made him feel tired, hopeless, and angry.

"Come on," she said softly.

Smiling inscrutably, she reached up and placed both her hands on the one he had around her neck. He was no longer applying any pressure. She slid the hand down to her naked breast, stretching her lips in a smoky smile. "Why don't we spend the day here, uh? Neither one of us really wants to go after

Hudson anymore. You've seen how he is. It is not reasonable. Besides" — she touched his fingers to a nipple — "you know you want me. What man doesn't want me — even one in love with his wife's ghost?"

He looked down at his hand on her full, firm breast. He pulled it away as though from something hot and, before he knew what he was doing, he slapped her with it. She gave a grunt as the blow whipped her head to the side.

She turned back to him slowly, a small cut on her lower lip leaking blood. Her smile had faded, but now it returned, mocking.

"No?" she said, spreading her knees and adding with a viper's allure, "Not even for free . . . for all you've done to help me get my gold back?" Her full upper lip curled in a sneer.

Rage burning inside him, he whipped his hand back to hit her again, but stopped. He lowered the hand and turned to the window, holstering his gun. He stared down at the muddy street, getting his temper under control.

After a time, she pulled on a wrapper and stood behind him at the window.

"You must have loved her very much," she said, not so much with sympathy but musingly, staring past his shoulder at the street.

"Not many men have refused me."

"Sorry to sully your run."

"Yes, at least I had that," she said with an ironic laugh. She moved forward and looked up at his face gravely, her guile and obstinance returning in a flash. "If you are still going after them, you crazy gringo," she said, enunciating each word with savage clarity, "then I am going with you."

"I thought you decided it wasn't 'reasonable.'"

"If you have not, I have not. It is worth the risk. Without the gold, I have nothing."

He looked down at her. She stared up at him with her round, brown eyes that had very little girlish innocence left in them. But there was some. At least enough to believe in buried treasure and in the myth that gold could make her happy.

He could think of no way short of torture to get her to tell him where Hudson was headed, and she'd already called his bluff once.

"You sure you know where he's going?"

"No."

Cuno frowned at her, his fury returning. She was playing him like a fiddle.

"Rick told me only that he hid the gold south of Wild Horse Basin."

"Wild Horse Basin?"

"You have not heard of it?"

"No."

"Then I guess you will need me to guide you. Not many know of it, and you will not find it on any map."

Cuno chuffed. "I reckon I don't have much choice, do I." He laughed mirthlessly. "Lady, you could drive me to violence."

She smiled and wrapped both hands around his bicep, squeezing. "Maybe later . . . under the stars, uh?"

He jerked his arm from her grasp. "Get dressed and meet me in the livery barn in twenty minutes."

He pushed brusquely past her as he strode through the door and clattered down the steps.

13

His face flushed with disgust, Ranger Jake Craig gigged his sorrel around a bend in the powdery trail. The sun blistered his cheeks and the sage tickled his nostrils, making him feel constantly on the verge of a sneeze.

"Goddamned locals don't give a rat's ass if a Ranger gets blown to a bloody pulp," he muttered, eyeing the horse prints gouging the sand and clay-colored dust beneath him. "If it had been one of their own, you think most of the posse would've hightailed it back to town?"

He grunted his own response.

Craig was still piss-burned because the posse that had headed out of Krantzburg with him last night, after he'd found the bloody body of his partner in the yard of Miss Kate's place, had turned tail and headed home after a storm had obliterated Hudson's tracks.

"Nothing against your partner, Jake," said Krantzburg's deputy marshal, Johnny Summerville, "but he had no business walking into Miss Kate's place alone like that, with no one to back his play." Summerville rode just behind Craig, on a long-legged steeldust. The deputy was tall, with a shock of dark hair covering his forehead beneath his wide-brimmed hat. He carried a double-barrel Greener, the shotgun's butt propped against his hip, and had an ivory-gripped Colt in a custom-tooled holster on his thigh.

Craig liked Summerville about as much as he'd like a .44 slug in the ass. The smug, cow-brained deputy bristled at taking orders from a Ranger, never mind that Craig had fought with the Confederacy when Summerville was still filling his britches with green goo. Craig could put up with a lot of things, but a snooty, snot-nosed local lawman whose dream was to read about himself in Eastern magazines was not one of those things.

"I mean," Summerville went on, "he left you a note sayin' he'd spotted the Hudson gang in town, right?"

"Yeah, he did," Craig allowed. It was true. Earl Diamond had left word at the front desk of Craig's hotel. But Earl hadn't bothered to wait till Craig, who'd been thumping a pretty Mexican whore, had received the message and gone to his partner's aid. Instead, Diamond had gone on over to Miss Kate's place by himself, no doubt because he'd been an infamous skinflint and hadn't wanted to share the reward money the gang had on its head with Craig.

Craig didn't voice his speculation to Johnny Summerville. True, Diamond was a skinflint, but he and Craig were partners. And out here, on the Arizona frontier, that meant something that neither Summerville nor any of the other locals could understand.

"But us Rangers protect you folks," Craig told the deputy, "and we deserve better backing than what the town marshal and the posse demonstrated last night."

"Well, I'm here," Summerville said, glancing at the six other posse members riding behind him. "Old Daddy's here . . . Walt's here . . . the teacher's here. . . ."

"Shut up," Craig said suddenly, reining his sorrel to a halt.

Summerville's tone was indignant. "What?"

"Is that fire?" Craig said, squinting across the rocky, sun-bleached wastes toward the column of black smoke unfurling about five miles away, above a scarp painted butter yellow by the three o'clock sun.

The rangy deputy followed Craig's gaze. "Could be Injuns."

"Could be," Craig said, trying to ignore the anger that galled his loins every time Summerville opened his mouth. "Could also be the men we're lookin' for."

As usual, Summerville was skeptical. "Doubt that. They've been headin' due south. The smoke's way west."

Again, Craig swallowed his anger. This shavetail had no respect for Rangers; that was a sad, frustrating fact. It wasn't so much what he said, but the tone in which he said it.

Saying nothing, Craig gigged his sorrel into a slow walk up the mesa, which had been pummeled and twisted by aeons of wind and unrelenting sun into bleached ridges and sand-blasted ravines. The trail was a slender game path sheathed in spindly desert shrubs and sand-mottled boulders.

"I sure don't like the idea of Injuns," one of the other posse members said behind Craig.

It was Cyril "Old Daddy" McCallister, who ran the express office. Old Daddy was a slender, gray-bearded raisin armed with a rusty cap-and-ball revolver, single-shot Cook & Brother rifle, and tarnished Green River knife he'd used when he'd first come west thirty years ago to trap beaver. For the occasion, he'd even dusted off his deer-hide hat, which had aged to the color of sun-bleached bone, and elk-skin leggings with holes in the knees.

"What'd you expect, Big Daddy?" Summerville said condescendingly. "This is Injun country, ain't it? Just keep your old eyes peeled and your old mouth shut."

Jake Craig felt like commanding the tin star to do the same, but kept silent as he rode. He contained his hatred of the deputy, staring at the smoke while looking for his best course up the gravelly mesa, letting his sorrel wend its way through occasional cedars and creosote shrubs.

The sun was a blazing iron on his face and neck. He felt his nose blistering. Cicadas whined loudly, giving a mocking, unrelenting voice to the heat. It wasn't unendurable, however, when Craig thought of the bounty on the heads of the Hudson gang. Page himself was worth two thousand dollars dead or alive. Craig had promised to split the money with the six posse members who had remained with him instead of following the hapless town marshal back to Krantzburg last night. But it still amounted to a sizable stake for, say, a gambling parlor in Prescott. . . .

Craig felt a little guilty, thinking of money

rather than revenge. But then, old Earl was a big boy. He knew the chance he was taking trying to squeeze Craig out of the bounty money.

"Try to spend it now, Earl," Craig grumbled.

"Where in the hell we goin', Craig?" Summerville said, his perpetual sneer twisting his brushy black mustache, his eyes flashing a sneer. "You sure you know this country? Maybe I should ride point."

He rode directly behind Craig, followed by the stagecoach messenger, Walter Greavis, Old Daddy McCallister, and the out-of-work drovers, Lewis Trotter and Wade Greenhill, who had thrown in with the posse while still drunk and whose faces now appeared pale as bird shit.

Bringing up the rear was the schoolteacher, Martin Plumb, who rode a white mare he'd rented from the livery barn. Clad in suit pants, string tie, and polished brogans, Plumb had made no bones about being deathly tired of teaching and wanting a stake for his own ranch. He was hoping the reward would make his dream possible at last.

"Check out that smoke there, lawman," Craig told Summerville, unable to conceal his disdain for the deputy any longer.

"Where's it look like I'm goin'?"

"You think it's Hudson, do you?"

"I have a feelin'."

Summerville thought about it a while. Apparently deciding Craig could be right, he gave a celebratory whoop. "What are you boys gonna do with your cuts?" he asked the others riding behind him. "Me, I'm gonna tell the marshal to kiss my ass, and I'm gonna run for county sheriff. Once I got that, I'm gonna ask Miss Angie to be my wife."

"Who?" Craig asked in spite of himself. He just couldn't stand the sound of Summerville's voice. If he had to be on the trail with the boy for very long, he knew he'd end up carving out his voice box with his barlow knife — slowly.

"Miss Angie Harmon," Summerville said, sticking his broad chest out like a peacock. "She's my betrothed, you might say. Her father is the biggest rancher in the county!"

"Betrothed, my ass!" cackled Old Daddy McCallister. "The day Ray Harmon lets his daughter marry you, Johnny my boy, is the day pigs'll start flyin' rings around the sun!"

Walt Greavis slapped his leg and threw his head back, guffawing. The others laughed, including the schoolteacher, who was known to be morose and taciturn when not drunkenly quoting English poetry in Krantzburg's saloons.

Craig turned to see Summerville, who scowled, lips pooched angrily, the black of his mustache standing out against his flush. Craig admonished the men to be quiet — they were in Apache country, for chrissakes — while grinning over his horse's ears.

God*damn,* he hated that kid! He entertained himself with the idea of drilling a bullet through the tin star on his chest, making it look like an accident. Who'd contest it?

It took the posse a good hour to wind down the other side of the mesa. They bottomed out in an ancient, boulder-strewn riverbed, and came upon tracks in the soft, wind-scalloped sand.

"Well, I'll be damned," Summerville said, leaning away from his horse to scour the ground with his fishy gaze. "The old Ranger's right. I recognize that toed-out hoofprint from the other side of the divide. It has to be one of Hudson's men."

"Why don't you talk a little louder!" Craig hissed. "Ole Geronimo's growin' hard of hearing!"

"Yeah, talk a little louder, you goddamn tinhorn," Greavis said, shoving his belligerent, unshaven face at the deputy.

"All of you shut up and follow me," Craig

whispered, feeling like the teacher of an unruly Sunday school class. "The smoke's rising just over that ridge yonder, and they could be leadin' us into a trap. Keep your eyes peeled and your weapons ready."

Craig moved out, and the others followed in a ragged line, riding slowly, watching the rocks and ridges around them. Keying on the thinning column of smoke, Craig crossed a wash and urged his sorrel up a low divide between two rocky buttes.

As the others spread out beside him, he gazed into the hollow in which a wagon and a small shack were burning. Flames licked up around the charred wagon bed and the logs of the cabin, which had been built against a cliff. The cabin's roof had collapsed, making the place little more than an ash heap.

Before the cabin lay two bodies — one facedown, arms and legs spread, the other on its side, face twisted back as if peering over its shoulder. A dead mule lay just beyond the dead men, its rounded belly dark with blood.

"That looks like Injun work," Summerville speculated.

"You're a lobo pup," Old Daddy grunted, keeping his voice down as he gazed into the hollow. "Injuns would've baked those men over the fire . . . after skinnin' 'em alive."

Ignoring the conversation, Craig shucked his saddle gun from its scabbard and hefted it meaningfully. "Who wants to ride down with me while the others stay here and cover us?"

"I do," Summerville said.

"That's what I was afraid of."

Craig looked at the others. He couldn't tell if the drovers were scared or sick with the bottle flu. They hadn't said anything except to each other for hours.

The teacher, Plumb, looked silently determined, sitting erect in his saddle, straw hat shading his scholarly face, sweat basting his striped, collarless shirt to his chest and flat belly. Old Daddy scowled down at the cabin and rolled a wad of chew from one side of his mouth to the other. The big rifle he held across his saddle bows belonged to another time.

Craig cocked his Winchester and looked at Summerville. "All right, but think before you do *anything,* and follow my lead."

The deputy only scowled at him.

"Let's go," Craig said, and kneed his horse down the hollow, taking it slow, running his gaze along the rocky slope on his right, then peering behind the cabin.

The flames were an opaque orange in the

bright sunlight, licking up around the blackened logs and white ashes heaped like snow. The fire was dying. Craig figured it had been set a couple of hours ago. That would be about right. He'd figured the gang to be about two hours ahead of the posse.

Nerves throughout his body crackled as he swung his gaze around absently, caressing his rifle trigger with a finger sweating inside a glove. The gang would be two hours ahead if they weren't lingering around here to ambush Craig's posse, that is.

He glanced at Johnny Summerville riding abreast of him, chin jutting. The kid was too stupid to be scared. From under the brim of his tall hat, he stared around at the rocks like he was looking for game.

Craig stopped the sorrel near the dead men. One had gray hair wisping around a pink pate. He'd fallen oddly, so that his bearded face stared back over his shoulder and up at the sky, teeth and eyes gleaming. What was left of his eyes, that is. The buzzards had already been feasting.

The other man had red-brown hair, bloody and matted where he'd been shot in the back of his head. He appeared to be somewhere in his late thirties. Both men were dressed in patched duck pants, suspenders, and low-heeled boots. Hard-rock miners, no doubt. They probably had a sluice box around here somewhere.

"Why do you s'pose Hudson killed these men?" Summerville said. It was the first time Craig had heard brittle uncertainty in the deputy's voice.

"For the fun of it probably." Craig was looking around at the rocks again, watching for movement or for a sun flash off a rifle barrel. At least, he hoped Hudson had shot the miners for the fun of it, and had not done all this killing and burning just to draw the posse in where he could get them all off his trail in one fell swoop.

The sun beat down brassily. A slight breeze spun a fine line of dust around the horses' hooves. It was a dragon's breath, offering no relief.

Craig walked his horse farther down the hollow, where he saw a mound of rubble and sluice boxes near a spring the miners had dug out of a wash. Their trash heap was nearby — a smelly collection of rotten food, cans, jars, and a few whiskey bottles, all strewn about by scavengers.

Seeing nothing fishy, Craig walked the sorrel back to the deputy, who had dismounted and was checking out the cabin. Craig waved to the rest of the posse up on the rocky knoll, and they filed down to join him — first

Plumb, then Greavis and Old Daddy, and then the drovers, picking their way down the rocky slope.

Craig heard a click. He jerked his head toward the slope opposite the cabin.

A stone rolled, coming to rest behind a boulder. A man stepped out from behind another boulder, aiming a rifle at the hollow.

Craig's heart skipped a beat. As he brought his own rifle up to his shoulder, he watched three more men step out from behind boulders and spindly shrubs, and raise rifles to their cheeks.

"Heyyyyy!"

The warning was a dry croak in Craig's throat, cut short by a staccato burst of gunfire. Craig had his gun up and was trying to settle a bead on one of the gang members when something ripped through his side, spinning him around and dropping him to his knees, the rifle leaping from his hands and clattering on the rocks.

He flailed there, trying to stand, hearing the shots and the bullets spanging off rocks and plunking into human flesh and horsehide, and the screams and yells of the posse members as they were blown out of their saddles.

Holding his side, Craig dropped to a shoulder and glanced toward the cabin.

Summerville was on a knee, levering his rifle as he returned fire and cursed. His curses stopped abruptly as bullets plunked through him, puffing dust from his clothes, his face becoming a bloody mask, his hat blown away. The deputy flew back with a scream, throwing his rifle, and Craig thought vaguely that maybe the kid really did have some sand in him — more sand than sense.

Quickly, the other yells died and were replaced by horse whinnies, rattling bridle chains, and clattering hooves and sifting dust.

Craig sucked air into his burning lungs and peered at the opposite slope, seeing little but powder smoke and dust. The squishing sound, he realized with horror, was his hand squeezing his own spilling innards.

"Don't kill the lawman!" someone yelled through the dust and smoke. "Don't kill him. Clevis, goddamnit, stay away from him. He's mine!"

Craig reached for his rifle, but it was too far away. He tried to draw his revolver, but his right arm — hell, his whole right side — was numb.

He stared through the smoke. Shadowy figures approached. Several crouched forward over rifle barrels. There was a big man holding a pistol; he tripped over a rock and angrily kicked it, then lifted his revolver and shot one of the drovers groaning to Craig's left.

A medium-tall man moved toward Craig through the dust, his features gradually focusing as if through a telescope lens. He aimed a rifle out from his hip. The man's light brown hair fell over his ears and collar. He wore a funneled hat trimmed with tin, and had two matching white scars on his sun-reddened cheeks. His small, deep-set eyes swam with insanity, their cold, black pupils fixed hungrily on Craig.

Page Hudson approached the Ranger. He stopped, placed a fist on a hip, and grinned as though at a long-lost pal.

"Hidy there, lawman. Boy, do I got some fun in store for you!"

14

Cuno and Marcella did not cut the posse's sign until late that day, several hours after the rain had quit and the sun had come out. They followed the meandering trail through the sun-scorched wasteland until dark.

While a lone lobo howled amongst the purple ridges, they made camp in a box canyon beneath ridges stippled with stunt cedars and Indian vetch. They set out early the next morning, following the posse's trail up a broad, rocky mesa.

Cuno figured they'd follow the trail as long as they had one. When and if they ran out of trail, Marcella would lead him to Wild Horse Basin. Cuno would track them from there.

Cuno rode Renegade, trailing a packhorse outfitted with trail supplies. Marcella rode her pinto, as moody and high-strung as she was. About ten o'clock that morning, Cuno saw the buzzards — black, winged specks over a distant butte. He shucked his Winchester from its boot and rode with the gun across his saddle bows. When he and Marcella topped the divide over the hollow, they reined their mounts to a halt and stared down.

Marcella shuddered audibly. Cuno's gut clenched. Below, several bodies and three horses lay twisted and strewn around the charred rubble of a burned-out cabin. Dark red blood stained the sand and cactus.

"Wait here," Cuno said.

Steering Renegade into the hollow, he peered around cautiously, his eyes lingering over the nine bodies lying in bloody heaps before the cabin and wagon, both of which were little more than white ash heaps and a few fire-blackened logs. The rocky ground was scored with hoofprints. Blood-splattered shell casings were strewn about like jackstraws. Cuno saw that the three horses he'd seen from the ridge were actually two horses and a mule.

But what attracted Cuno's eyes over and over again as he rode slowly amidst the carnage was a curved saber sticking, blade up, out of the ground, a few feet from one of the dead horses. Impaled upon the tip was a human head — eyes bulging, tongue pro-

191

truding, yellow teeth glistening. The face was gaunt and pale as porcelain. Curly gray hair lay matted flat to the scalp and was crawling with flies.

Lying nearby was a headless body, arms outspread, one boot crossed over a knee. The torso was so matted with blood that Cuno could barely make out the Arizona Rangers badge pinned to the deer-hide vest.

The girl walked her horse up behind him. Both mounts spooked at the grisly sight, sidestepping and flicking their ears. Finally, the girl galloped off, stopped her horse several yards away, and jumped out of the saddle. Cuno heard her retch.

After briefly inspecting the other bullet-riddled bodies, Cuno estimated that most of the men had been dead since late yesterday afternoon. He rode over to the girl. She was drinking water from her canteen, facing away from the carnage and the loudly buzzing flies.

She turned to Cuno, her face ashen. "Page Hudson is a savage." Her lip curled back upon itself. "Why did he cut off the man's head?"

"To warn anyone else thinking about following them," Cuno said, slipping his canteen strap over his saddle horn. "That'd be my guess."

He took a long drink, washing down his own bile. When he lowered the canteen, he glanced at the impaled head again. "Sure you don't wanna just tell me where Hudson's headed? Might save you a lot of misery."

She sniffed and wiped her hand across her mouth. When she'd hung her canteen back on her saddle, she opened her saddlebags and produced her six-shooter, holster, and cartridge belt. She wrapped the rig around her slender waist, tongued the flap, and cinched it.

"I have seen evidence before of Hudson's savagery." Her gun and holster looked too big on her. As she toed a stirrup and swung up onto her horse, the pistol interfered with her movements. "Let's go."

They rode hard through the desert wastes, trailing the packhorses and following Hudson's sign, which the gang had done nothing to hide. It was tough, hot going, and Cuno saw the wear on the girl's face. He could tell by the way she fidgeted on her saddle that her backside was getting sore. Still, she did not complain or slow her pace.

By the end of that day, Cuno judged by the tracks that they had closed the gap between themselves and the outlaws by several miles. The gang might have been only a few miles away. There was a high, small moon, and after stopping for a brief supper of hardtack and jerky washed down with water, they continued riding by moonlight.

Even by moonlight, night riding was dangerous in this country, with deep ravines and canyons opening around them, but Cuno felt a steely, barely contained rage spurring him onward. His desire to close the gap between himself and the killers became more of an obsession with every clattering step of Renegade's hooves. By midnight, however, the mounts were too tired to go any farther. Reluctantly, Cuno and Marcella made camp in a boulder nest halfway up a flame-shaped scarp, with a spring murmuring up from a cairn of mossy stones.

"How far away do you think they are now?" Marcella asked. She smoothed her sweat-damp hair back from her temples as she sat near the small fire Cuno had built from the nearly smokeless branches of a curl leaf shrub.

"By their tracks I'd say two hours. Three at the most."

"We will catch up to them tomorrow?" Sitting Indian-style, she held a tin cup of coffee before her. Her cotton shirt, unbuttoned below her neck to the cooling breeze, was dirty and crusted from dried sweat. Her hair was disheveled, her cheeks streaked with dust.

Blowing ripples on his coffee, Cuno said, "That's what I figure."

"And then what?"

"Then we watch 'em for a while, trail 'em, maybe get ahead and set up an ambush."

Her eyes widened slightly, brightening at the prospect. *"Sí . . ."*

They'd rolled into their blankets, using their saddles for pillows, when they heard the sound of a stone rolling followed by a slender twig snapping. The four picketed horses snorted a warning and pulled at their ropes.

Inhaling sharply, Marcella jerked her head up. Cuno grabbed his Colt from the holster coiled around his saddle horn.

"Shhh," he said. "Stay here."

He kicked sand on the fire's glowing remains. Then he slipped into his boots and, revolver in hand, stole away from the camp.

Bringing his boots down quietly in the sand and gravel, he walked around boulders, gradually working his way up the escarpment. He paused near a cedar, frozen and listening, hearing only the slight breeze folding around the upthrusting stone and whistling softly in a distant hollow, nudging the cedar's branches.

On the breeze he detected a faint, musky smell, like the odor of scraped animal plew left to sweeten in the sun. Indians often smelled that way. Cougars and mountain lions did too.

He thumbed back the Colt's trigger and edged around a boulder, ducking under the branches of a pine growing through a crack in the escarpment. Shortly, he came to a shelf a foot above him. There was a V-shaped crack in the middle of the shelf. He was about to climb through when two gold eyes blazed atop the shelf's rim.

Silhouetted against the stars, a tufted tail whipped like a blacksnake.

The black shape of the cat plunged toward him, paws forward, an angry wail bursting from its throat. Cuno fired. As he sailed backward, his right arm and hand burned and throbbed. Then everything went numb as his head hit the rock slab, his vision dimming.

Vaguely, he heard another snarl. He smelled the pungent, urinelike odor of the cat as it leaped to its feet, sprang off its back legs, and disappeared somewhere above his field of vision — a silent, leaping shadow.

He forced himself onto his chest and grabbed the Colt. Thumbing back the hammer, he waited in case the cat returned. The pine needles stabbed his chest like broken glass. His heart leapt against his ribs, and his breath came fast. His gun butt was slick from the cut the cat had opened in his hand.

Something moved to his right. Jerking toward it, he grunted at the pain shooting through his hand and arm.

"It's me," the girl said, breathless. She stood on the other side of a shallow trough, moonlight winking off the receiver of Cuno's rifle in her hands. "What was it — cat?"

"Painter. Must've been after the horses."

Holstering his gun, Cuno climbed to his knees. His shirt was blood-soaked and his right hand screamed with pain. He couldn't see much in the dark, but he knew the cat had opened him up. His head pounded from the fall.

"How bad are you hurt?" Marcella asked him. "Is that your shooting hand?"

He raised his arm, trying to flex his hand, but it felt like the muscles had been cut deep. "Son of a bitch!"

He walked back to the camp and threw several chunks of curl-leaf on the fire with his good hand. When the flames licked up, revealing the camp with its tack, panniers, burlap sack of cooking utensils, and disheveled blankets, he sat on a rock and unbuttoned the cuff of his shirt sleeve. Propping his elbow on his thigh, he carefully rolled the sleeve back from his forearm, wincing against the sting.

"Fill the wreck pan with water," he told the girl.

She'd crouched beside him and was studying his bloody hand and arm. The cat's claws had cut two jagged lines from his middle knuckle to his wrist. A third gash ran from his thumb straight across his hand. The skin around the cuts looked tattered as torn burlap. *"Madre Maria!"* she exclaimed. "Now what are we going to do? Can you shoot with your left hand?"

"Just get me the goddamn water!"

Turning away, she slapped her hands against her thighs with disgust. "I am in Apache country with a cripple!"

"Your concern is heartwarming," he said, inspecting his bloody arm.

When she'd filled the tin bowl with water, she set it on a flat stone by the fire. Cursing under his breath, he bathed the arm and hand in the bowl, wincing as he cleaned the cuts.

He found himself sharing the girl's exasperation. He wouldn't be shooting with the hand for a good long time. With Hudson only a few miles ahead. The thought turned his stomach raw.

It must have done the same thing to Marcella. When he'd finished wrapping his arm with an old shirt from his saddlebags, he looked around and saw her sitting against her saddle, boots crossed, angrily sipping whiskey from a bottle and eyeing him with disgust.

He picked up his rifle, inspected the action, then grabbed the bottle from her hands.

"I need that worse than you do," he grumbled.

Then he headed into the darkness to keep watch for Indians and any more goddamn cats.

15

"It seems like we been ridin' forever," Clevis O'Malley complained as he rode lazily atop his short-legged dun, trailing a dapple-gray packhorse on a lead rope. "How the hell much further we have anyways?"

"You only been ridin' three days, Cleve," Page Hudson said. They were riding single file, Hudson in the lead, O'Malley behind him. Two lumbering pack mules followed Saber and Wilks on lead lines. "I figure we got two, three more . . . everything goes all right."

"Page, what'd you say the name o' this place was we're headed for?" Kenny Wilks asked. He was feeling much better now that his arm was healing. The riding had badgered him at first, but now the dry sun had worked its magic. He wasn't worrying so much about blood poisoning anymore.

"Wild Horse."

"Wild Horse?"

"That's what he said, didn't he?" Billy Saber rode third in line, Wilks behind him. "Drain the piss outta your ears, Kenny."

"Shut up, Billy."

"Shut up your ownself, or—"

"Boys, boys," Hudson said, raising a placating hand without turning around. "That's enough tail-twisting."

"Sorry, Page," Saber said. "He gets on my nerves, that's all. Damn crybaby . . . weepin' over that bullet burn. Pshaw! I been shot so many times my ma liked to mistake me for a sieve. You didn't hear me bawlin' about it." Saber snugged his Confederate cap down to keep the blistering sun off his ears.

"My family's prone to infection!" Wilks complained. "And if you call me any more names, you son of a bitch—"

"Boys!" Hudson yelled, craning around in his saddle. "If I have to tell you one more time to quit hoorawing each other, I'm gonna ride back there and do some hoorawin' of my own." He turned his livid gaze to Saber riding behind O'Malley. "Billy, you have a beef with Kenny, just remember how fast he is with that hogleg."

Clevis shook his head. "It's true," the big Irishman said, chewing a twist from a tobacco braid. "I remember two years ago, little Kenny shot a deputy U.S. marshal in front of the Republican Saloon in Wichita. Two bullets right through the heart before the badge-toter even had his gun out of his holster."

"So there you have it," Hudson told Saber.

Kenny Wilks grinned as he rode, relaxing now and swaying in his saddle. The wiry, towheaded whelp, whose pallid face was peeling from sunburn, kept his hand glued to his pistol. The brim of his oversized bowler carried a pound of desert sand kicked up by the horses.

Billy Saber squinted his pale eyes skeptically at Hudson, stretching his lips away from his crooked front teeth. "I don't believe it."

"If you don't believe it," Wilks suggested smugly, "why don't you and me have us a little lead-swappin' contest."

Saber turned to look at the diminutive kid, who looked and talked like a range-bred Kansas cow waddie.

"Save it, Kenny," Hudson said. "Shootin' might draw Apaches." Besides, he thought, he needed all three of these men to help get him to Wild Horse. If Apaches showed, he'd need all the guns he could get.

As soon as he'd made it to Tucson, these men could perforate each other all they wanted, for all Hudson cared. It would save him from having to use his own ammunition.

They rode for another hour, the horses clomping along on the stony ground, the sun angling overhead. Stony ridges and shelves rose around them, with here and there distant mountain ranges lolling against the liquid horizon. Occasionally they saw a hawk riding a thermal, or a roadrunner would make a red splash across their trail. But mostly they saw only rocks and orange caliche between cactus patches.

"How come I never heard of no town called Wild Horse, Page?" O'Malley asked as they rode through a dusty wash in which the bones of a dead fawn lay strewn.

"'Cause it never was much of a town," Hudson said, glancing casually at the bones. "It boomed and collapsed in pret' near the same year. Rick tried to mine there before we pulled the stage job and came up with the gold. Guess he figured it wasn't too far from our pa's ranch, and he'd be able to find it again easy enough . . . once he got shed of me."

"Sure is awful when a brother double-crosses a brother," O'Malley said mournfully. "Ain't natural."

"Yeah, well, we were only half brothers, and I used to beat the shit out of Rick all the time we was growin' up. Pa never cared. He never cared for Rick neither."

"Your pa still ranch there, Page?" Billy Saber asked. They were climbing out of the wash through spindly aspens, and entering a narrow valley.

Hudson shook his head. "The old bastard died in the privy the year after the robbery. Reckon his heart couldn't take the shame of havin' two sons turn owlhoot, and then one killin' the other." He paused. "Or maybe my stepma told him what I did to her."

O'Malley, Wilks, and Saber shared dubious looks. Finally, Saber said with a tentative air, "W-what'd you do to her, Page?"

Hudson hipped around in his saddle to stare at the others, smiling wickedly. "Nothin' she wasn't askin' for, the way she used to dress for a woman her age."

Hudson winked and turned back around.

O'Malley snickered. Saber grinned thoughtfully as he rode. Kenny Wilks shook his head. "You'd have to pay me a lot of *dinero* before I'd slip it to my stepma," he said. "I mean, *a lot!*"

"Shut up!" Hudson rasped suddenly, jerking his arm down for silence. He pulled on his reins, and the horse lifted its head back from the bit.

No one said anything as the horses ground

to a halt. "What is it?" O'Malley said softly, following Hudson's sweeping gaze around the rocky ridges abutting both sides of the valley.

The slopes were several hundred feet high, and the west-angling sun brushed them with copper.

"See that big rock over there on that hill? The big one looks like the hull of a ship? I seen a shadow slip behind it."

"Shit," Saber whispered, drawing his mount abreast of Hudson and O'Malley.

"Indians?" Wilks asked, drawing his revolver.

"Put your gun away," O'Malley told him. When Wilks only frowned, pistol in hand, Clevis jerked his head angrily. "Now! Put it away."

Reluctantly, Wilks holstered his six-shooter.

They were all looking at O'Malley now, puzzled. "If that's Apaches up there — and who else could it be? — it's best not to look too eager for a fight."

"Okay," Hudson said after a time. "So what do we do?"

O'Malley ran a gloved hand through his shaggy, dusty beard, cuffed his high-crowned hat back off his forehead, and gently kneed his horse forward. "We ride slow . . .

real casual-like. And don't nobody get the trigger itch. Only shoot if you're fired at."

Hudson was dubious. He'd grown up in Apache country and was aware of the Indians' threat, but he figured O'Malley, who'd made a living out of fighting the savages, knew what he was talking about. The big Irishman had tangled with plenty of Apaches when he'd hunted their scalps along the border, before the army had thrown him in the sweat box for selling stolen army remounts in Mexico and for sundry other sins he rarely talked about unless inspired by sour mash.

Bowing to O'Malley's experience, Hudson gave him the lead, slipping in behind him, riding abreast of Saber. The horses rode slowly through the canyon, the clip-clops of the hooves echoing as the ridges narrowed around them. A jackrabbit scurried across the trail and disappeared into a hole between two boulders. The hair on the back of Hudson's neck pricked, but he saw nothing until they were halfway through the canyon.

Then, out of nowhere, on the north-facing slope only fifty feet to Hudson's right, a short figure appeared atop a boulder, crouching like a cat about to spring. To this man's left, another figure stepped casually out from behind another rock.

As O'Malley sawed back on his horse's reins, two more Indians appeared, hunkering atop rocks on the other side of the canyon. Their red bandannas, calico shirts, and long, obsidian hair whipped in the breeze. Most held bows notched with arrows. Two held spears.

"Easy, boys," O'Malley said in a low, flinty voice. "You wanna die right quick, just reach for your irons."

"Ah, shit," Billy Saber groaned.

"Shut up," Hudson said. He smiled up at the ridges, where the short, dark figures stood staring down at them coldly. He'd heard all his life that one thing you never showed an Indian was fear.

The wind whipped through the canyon. One of the Indians was so close, Hudson could hear the man's stolen cavalry pants fluttering against his legs. It was this man who spoke, gesturing with his left hand. To Hudson the clipped grunts and guttural spats made no sense at all. Listening intently, O'Malley seemed to understand.

When the Indian stopped talking, the Irishman spoke in what sounded like the Indian's own nonsensical tongue, his face flushing with frustration as he flailed mentally for the words he needed.

After the Indian had spoken again, O'Malley turned to Hudson. "They want our pack mules."

Hudson grimaced. "Tell 'em to diddle themselves!"

O'Malley stared at him. "We don't give 'em the mules, there's gonna be a fight."

"So what? There's four o' them and four o' us."

"Uh-uh," O'Malley returned. "Look up yonder."

Hudson followed the Irishman's gaze down the canyon. He counted at least six more Indians perched atop the rocks along the trail, looking this way.

"Ah, shit!" Saber groaned again.

"Billy, if you don't shut up I'm gonna cut your ears off and hang 'em around my neck," Hudson growled, staring darkly down canyon.

"I say we give 'em the mules," Kenny Wilks said quietly, his baggy suit coat flapping in the wind. "That gold ain't gonna do us any good if we're too dead to spend it. Besides, you ever see Apache torture tricks?"

"Shut up, Kenny," Hudson said in a low voice trimmed with menace. To O'Malley he said, "How come they didn't just ambush us?"

"'Cause we're well-armed and we look

like border roughs," O'Malley said, a grin lifting the beard on his sun-mottled cheeks. "They probably been losing warriors in army fights of late, and can't afford to lose any more. They need food bad and would rather get it the easy way."

"If we turn over the mules, you think they'll really let us pass?"

The big man pawed his beard. "Usually an Injun's word is good. If they wanted a fight, I'd say we'd already be fightin'."

Hudson thought it over as he stared at the round-faced Indian nearest their trail. Dried, crusty blood streaked both legs of the dusty, blue cavalry pants.

Fingering one of the two white scars on his face, Hudson glanced at Wilks. "Turn the mules loose, Kenny."

Wilks slipped his knife from his belt sheath, turned in his saddle, and cut the mules loose from his horse's tail. Dumbly, the mules just stood there, blinking, their withers occasionally rippling at flies.

Clevis spit a few phrases at the Apache leader. For several seconds, the Apache just stood there as though carved from stone. Then, his face expressionless, he threw an arm out, indicating the trail down the canyon.

"I reckon we can go," O'Malley said.

"Let's go, boys . . . nice and slow," Hudson told Wilks and Saber.

"Keep your hands away from your guns and your chins up," O'Malley advised. "Don't look scared."

"Hell," Billy Saber snarled. "I ain't afraid o' these red devils."

Slowly, the four outlaws made their way down the canyon, watching the Indians standing on the rocks around them. The Indians stared dully, holding their notched bows in their hands. Hudson eyed them, smiling a thin smile, trying to look bold, riding with both hands on the reins.

Thieving, stinking dog-eaters. If he and his boys weren't outnumbered, these savages would know what hot lead felt like. . . .

After an eternity, they reached the opening of the canyon. Two Apaches stood there, one on either side of the trail. One was an old man, judging from the deep lines in his face and the heavy bags under his eyes. The other was a young brave, no more than fifteen. He was several inches taller than the old man, but he still wasn't over six feet. He carried a bow and had an arrow quiver, and an old-model Navy Colt protruded from his sash.

As he approached the pair, Hudson shuttled his gaze from one to the other. Then he passed between them and turned his gaze ahead, feeling his back tingle, waiting for an arrow.

"Billy, Kenny — you two still back there?"

"We're back here, Page," Kenny replied. "Looks like we made it."

"Just keep riding," O'Malley said, leading the procession down a steep grade and onto a desert flat. A broad expanse of creosote and greasewood opened before them. An oceanlike mirage fluttered on the horizon. Saguaros dipped and rolled like ships at sea.

Several minutes later, O'Malley reined his horse to a halt and quartered around in the trail. The others did likewise, gazing behind them at the blue cleft in the mountain through which they'd just passed. Seeing no Apaches storming after them, Hudson heaved a long sigh of relief.

"Glad that's over."

"Me too." Wilks rubbed his arm, which tension had caused to grow sore again.

"Thieving bastards," Saber said, angrily digging his makings sack from his shirt pocket. "If I ever catch an Indian out alone someplace, I'm gonna cut his innards out and wrap 'em around his neck!"

"Well, we know one thing," O'Malley said.

Hudson looked at him. "What's that?"

"If anybody's still trailin' us, they won't be for long. Ain't no more white-eyes gettin' through that canyon." The dark-bearded man shook his head. "Uh-uh. Not a chance!"

"Who in the hell would be back there anyway?" Kenny Wilks said. "We done finished off that posse. And that town marshal ain't gonna trouble himself."

"I was thinkin' Massey," Clevis said. "That boy's got a mad on for us."

Hudson grunted a laugh. "Not even that trigger-itchy squaw-dog would be fool enough to trail us through 'Pache country." He reined his horse past O'Malley, retaking his lead. "Come on, boys. We're flappin' our jaws and burnin' daylight."

16

Cuno's hand was wrapped tightly to keep it from bleeding. It grieved him, but the pain wasn't as bad as knowing the hand was virtually useless. The deep cut had tightened the muscles and made gripping a pistol butt impossible.

When he had to shoot, he'd have to use his left hand. That meant he'd have to take down the Hudson gang one at a time. That meant, in turn, that he'd have to get them separated somewhere.

The second night after his tussle with the cat, he and Marcella camped near a sump in a dry creek bed. Galleta grass rimmed the blue-green pool, which smelled faintly of alkali. Cuno built a small fire and brewed coffee, and they ate a rabbit he'd snared.

"So, what about this gold?" he asked her conversationally as she scrubbed their dishes in the wreck pan. He'd sunk back against his saddle and was awkwardly rolling a smoke with his good hand.

She looked at him sharply, her round eyes flashing in the firelight. "What about it?"

"Don't worry," he said, twisting the misshapen cylinder. "I'm not interested in acquiring any of it. It's stolen, I take it. I'm just wondering where it came from and how you come to find out about it."

She'd stopped scrubbing. "Why should I tell you?"

Cuno struck a match and lit the cigarette, blowing smoke out the side of his mouth. He shrugged a shoulder. "Okay, don't. Just thought we'd make a little conversation."

"Why are you so interested in the gold all of a sudden?"

"Forget it." He stretched a leg out and kicked a log down in the fire.

"I suppose you feel you're entitled to some? Because you're going to kill Hudson for me."

His eyes narrowed. "Listen, lady," he said, "when I kill Hudson it ain't gonna be for you or any goddamn gold. Don't you forget that. I don't give a shit about your gold."

Her eyes blazed for a moment, then dropped to the wreck pan. Slowly, thoughtfully, she continued scrubbing a skillet.

After a while she spoke. "Page and his brother, Rick, rode in the same gang for a while. I was Rick's woman. A year ago, they robbed a stagecoach and found gold bars in the strongbox. The group separated — Page taking half the men, Rick taking the other half — because they knew a large posse would be after them. Rick took the gold with him and double-crossed Page."

"He hid the gold?"

"*Sí.* He wanted the law to settle down before he and his men tried making a run for *Méjico.*" Marcella set the skillet aside to dry, and sighed with resignation. "His mistake was visiting me in Prescott. Page was waiting for him. He killed Rick after he tortured him, and I ran away in the night."

"You were afraid Hudson figured you knew where the gold was hid?"

She nodded. "Only a few days ago, in the roadhouse, I learned that Rick had hidden a map to the gold in my mother's silver crucifix. I had been carrying the map for a year and didn't know it."

Cuno smiled wryly as he lay back on his elbows and blew cigarette smoke at the stars. "Hudson knew it, because he tortured the information out of Rick. . . ."

"*Sí.*" She bared her lips in a snarl as she stood and tossed the wash water into the willows, making the horses jump. "And he took it."

"And now you're gonna get it back . . . or die trying."

"And why should I not?" she said, turning to him with self-righteous fire in her eyes. "Rick died for that money. He . . . he would want me to have it."

Unmoved, Cuno flicked his cigarette into the fire. "'Cause it ain't yours."

She laughed without mirth. "Who are you to judge? Mr. Vigilante with his smoking guns. Ha!"

"Maybe, but I'd die before I whored myself like you've done, then pissed and moaned about it like I'd had no choice in the matter."

She stood staring down at him, her nostrils flaring, her eyes glinting like sun-struck coal.

"Bastard!" she cried, plucking a knife off a rock. "Bastard!" She bolted toward him, swinging the knife.

He reached up and caught her wrist a foot away from his neck. In the same motion, he kicked her feet out from under her and threw her onto her back. She screamed and kicked, tossing her head like an animal, her hair flying over her face.

"Bastard . . . I'll kill you!"

He climbed on top of her, pinning her arms down with his hands. He squeezed her wrist until her hand opened, and the knife fell into the grass.

"No!" she cried, and followed it up with a string of Spanish even he, with his limited understanding of the language, recognized as an unfavorable assessment of his lineage.

He slapped her with his open palm. That shut her up. She stared up at him, her eyes slowly losing their fire, her exposed cleavage rising and falling as she breathed. A funny smile quirked her lips, curling the upper one characteristically.

"You do like it rough, eh?" she said in a throaty, lusty voice. She ground her groin against his and touched the tip of her tongue to her lip. "Well, then, what are you waiting for . . . ?"

She lifted her head to kiss him, but he jerked his own head away. Slowly, holding her gaze, he pushed onto his knees, from his knees to his feet.

Breathing heavily, he turned away from her, walked over to a tree, and sat down.

Giving a throaty, mocking laugh, she got up and straightened her clothes. She looked at him again with that funny smile, ran her hand over her mouth, then turned abruptly and walked away toward the pool. In a moment, he heard water splashing softly as she washed.

Sitting with his back to the tree, he adjusted his bandage on his hand. He felt sheepish about insulting her, but not enough to apologize. What had angered him most, he realized now, was that she'd had a point. He'd been raised well enough to know that vengeance was no less a sin than thievery and greed. Turn the other cheek and all that bullshit. But it did nothing to soften his resolve to kill without mercy, to even the score.

With a sigh, he reclined against his saddle and lowered his hat over his eyes. He needed to sleep. He had a feeling tomorrow would be a big day. He knew Marcella well enough to know that her fire had died and that she was no longer a danger — an immediate one anyway.

She returned to the fire a few minutes later, her hair and face shining with the water she'd used to sponge away the trail dust. Her shirttails hung out of her men's blue jeans. Stopping near Cuno, she opened her mouth to speak, then stopped.

He was sleeping, soft snores escaping his slightly parted lips.

Marcella gave an angry snort, walked over to her bedroll, and picked up a towel. She turned to him, frowning, as she toweled the water from her face and hair. She unbuttoned her damp shirt and toweled her breasts and, still watching him, found her disdain turning to frustration.

Why did he never look at her the way most men did? Most men wanted her the moment they laid eyes on her, their eyes flattening as they lingered over her body with cool appraisal inevitably turning to a flinty lust.

She had grown to hate that look — or she'd thought she had. But the absence of Cuno Massey's admiration and approval had her wondering.

Then she wondered why she'd been wondering. Had she become attracted to him?

She studied him now, her arms hanging at her sides, remembering how his weight had felt atop her, his bulging groin against hers, his powerful hands pinning hers to the ground.

He was a big, capable man. Young, but she'd known older men much younger than him. His legs were long, his thighs round with sculpted muscles, as were his arms. The hands laced together on his chest were hammy and red-brown from the sun. Clay was ground into his callused fingertips, making coppery half-moons under the nails. His heavy chin jutted from beneath his hat, and his blond hair was getting long, hanging well over his collar and curling slightly.

She found her eyes straying beneath his wide, brown belt, to the faded denim bulging over his crotch. Her face warming with both desire and shame, she sank to her knees, but kept looking at him as she slowly reclined against her saddle.

Most of the men she'd known had exuded a brute power propelled by animal lust and greed. They were savage men — angry, capricious, and evil. She had never known any other kind of man, including the gambler.

Cuno puzzled her, evoking emotions in herself totally foreign to her.

As she lay gazing at him, she wondered what it would be like to lay engulfed by those heavy arms, encased in those rounded shoulders. How mild and knowable the world might seem, if only for a few minutes. How safe she would feel. . . .

And then she felt another, startling emotion: jealousy for a dead woman she had never known and who still inspired a passion in this man, a passion like Marcella Jiminez had never felt nor witnessed in another.

She turned her back to Cuno Massey.

Oh, but she did feel a passion as real as any other. She felt a passion for the gold.

Unexpectedly, the notion saddened her.

Frowning, she turned onto her side and curled her knees. She drew her blanket up and fell asleep cupping her naked breasts in her hands.

His face buried in his hat, Cuno was dreaming.

In the dream he, July, and Vera Grissom were dancing to Farley Grissom's fiddle during a Friday night get-together in the Masseys' new cabin. It was a three-person hoedown of sorts, and Cuno swung each girl in turn. Releasing Vera, he danced a jig around the plank table as the women clapped time while Farley stomped his foot. Cuno grabbed July, swung her high in the air, and kissed her on the way down.

"Cuno Massey," she cajoled him, laughing with embarrassment, "not in front of the neighbors!"

"Go ahead, boy — we ain't lookin'!" Farley said with a whoop as he fiddled.

But by then Cuno was hooking his left arm through Vera's right and swinging her about in front of the fireplace in which an iron stew pot bubbled.

In the dream, time sped up, and he and July were telling the Grissoms good-bye and watching them ride away in their rattling wagon, fading into the darkness beyond the hollow. Crickets and frogs sang the starry night alive.

At home, Cuno turned to July in the open doorway. She stood silhouetted by the hurricane lamp on the table behind her. He moved to her, saw her smoky, alluring gaze, strands of black hair pasted to her cheeks still moist from their dancing.

"Fun tonight," he said, still feeling light and energetic from Grissom's plum wine, the good food, and the laughter. He hadn't felt so good or so at home anywhere since his father and stepmother were killed in Nebraska.

"Cuno," July said in a breathy voice, taking his hands in hers and staring up at him, her brown eyes wide and filled with a hushed, barely restrained glee, "do you love me?"

He smiled, squeezing her hands. "I'll say I do."

"Then take me." She said it with a shiver, throwing her arms around his neck, pulling him down to her and kissing him, her mouth open, tongue probing, her breasts growing hard against his chest.

At last, she pulled away from him, breathing heavily. His own desire awakened and burning deep within him, Cuno bent down, picked her up in his arms, and carried her into their bedroom off the kitchen. He undressed her slowly, savoring each moment, pausing to kiss her and to run his hands along her naked flesh, probing every inch of her slender, butter-smooth body with his fingers.

Then he got up, undressed before her as she lay watching and breathing audibly.

And then she touched him, worked him into a frenzy with her hands, and gently guided him between her legs.

"Cuno," she whispered, nibbling his ear as he moved against her, "I know we're going to make a beautiful baby."

He lifted his hand, ran his fingers along her cheek. "July . . ."

Then his eyes were open and he found himself staring into the darkness relieved by an umber fire's glow, propped on his hands. His hat had tumbled into his lap.

He must have said something in his sleep. Marcella opened her eyes and lifted her head, blinking at him sleepily. Realizing he'd been dreaming, she shook her head slowly and lay back against her saddle.

"No," she said with a fateful sigh. "You are alone . . . just as I am alone . . . All alone."

Cuno blinked his eyes and swung his head around searchingly. It was true. He could still feel the moist skin along July's cheek, the plump swell of her lips under his exploring fingers. July was as real to him as his own heartbeat, but she wasn't here. She would never be here again. . . .

He sat there as the familiar emptiness and grief washed over him as if for the first time, like a physical weight bearing down on him, leaving him nearly breathless. His heart raced, his knees and feet ached. Sweat popped out on his forehead.

After a while, returning his mind to the present through a sheer force of will, he forced away the grief enough to make breathing possible again.

He climbed to his feet as heavily as an old man, picked up his rifle, and headed off to scout around the camp.

17

"We're gaining on them," Cuno said the next morning. He hunkered down on his haunches and ran two fingers of his left hand along a faint hoofprint scoring the flinty clay. A hot wind had picked up when he and Marcella had broken camp. It blew now, nudging the sand around the hoofprint.

"How far away do you think they are?"

"Judging by their tracks, I'd say we'll catch up to them tonight or early tomorrow."

He glanced around at the sage-tufted tables rising around him. Sun-blasted monoliths rose in the south. Through these jagged dinosaur teeth the killers' trail twisted, rising over a grade behind which Cuno could see only a vast yellow sky splotched with crimson.

Staring at that ominous hell-sky and imagining how it would be killing the first of the Hudson gang — poking a barrel against the man's temple and pulling the trigger — he became aware of a hot wind blowing through him as well as without, anticipation twitching his injured right hand and making his spine burn.

He stood quickly and toed a stirrup. In a moment, he and Marcella were cantering their horses up the grade — two mounted riders silhouetted against the crimson hell-sky that appeared to pulse and throb, gradually expanding as though fed by a building storm.

They rode with renewed vigor. They stopped only twice to water their horses, but late in the afternoon, faint pistol pops sounded. Cuno sawed back on his reins and looked around, one hand on his revolver's butt.

In the northeast, about a thousand yards away, a thin dust crown rose. Squinting against the sun glare and shading his eyes with his other hand, Cuno made out an inky red stagecoach at the crown's head. The Conestoga fishtailed around a rimrock behind six frantic horses chewing up the ground with terrified abandon, their ears laid flat against their heads.

The driver cracked a blacksnake over the team's backs while the shotgun messenger craned around in his seat and fired his coach gun from his shoulder. The shotgun's deep roars momentarily drowned out the snaps of the revolvers that the passengers fired out the coach windows.

In a moment, Cuno saw the reason for the wild ride.

At least a dozen Apaches were bearing down on the stagecoach from behind, loosing arrows and tossing spears, their short-legged pinto ponies galloping so fast they were mere blurs in the dust kicked up by the coach's team and its iron-rimmed wheels.

An Apache rushing up beside the coach threw a spear. The messenger had breeched his shotgun to reload, and the spear plowed through his chest. Cuno saw the man fall back against the driver, who was still cracking the whip over the team's backs.

The messenger crouched over the spear. A moment later, he tumbled down from the driver's box and disappeared under the wheels and the attacking Indians' thundering hooves.

There were several more shots, and then the stage bucked, fishtailing violently as it disappeared behind another rimrock. Cuno heard the horses scream and the Indians whoop, and then there was an eerie, spine-splintering sound like wood snapping.

"Damn it all!" Cuno said, more annoyed

by another delay than concerned about the stage passengers. To Marcella, he said, "Wait here," and gigged Renegade into a gallop toward the rimrock.

He galloped a serpentine course around the sage tufts and boulders, tracing a wide semicircle around the rimrock. He crossed a dry wash, traversed a knoll, and leapt a natural levee. The rimrock fell back on his right, revealing clay-colored dust broiling up from the sage and low-growing desert trees.

He could hear the Indians' whoops and a pistol's erratic pops. A woman screamed. He couldn't see much more than a few moving figures and dust.

He reined his paint to a stop. The horse blew and sidestepped, fearful of the Indians' hellish cacophony. The woman screamed again. Peering into the dust, Cuno dismounted, tied Renegade to a mesquite shrub, and shucked his Winchester.

He walked through the shrubs, keeping his head low. When the woman's screams and the Indians' frenzied cries sounded only a hundred or so yards away, he made for a low escarpment rising on his right. Climbing it, the woman's screams setting his teeth to grinding, he hunkered behind a rectangular, flat-topped boulder and cast his gaze into the flat below.

The stage lay on its side as though dropped from the sky. The horses had broken away and were gone. From this distance — about seventy yards — Cuno could see the Indians milling around the stage, loosing arrows and spears as they finished off the passengers. Some of the attackers were mounted, several were not. Those not savaging the passengers were tearing through the strewn luggage.

As the dust thinned, Cuno saw several bodies scattered amongst the sage. Several yards behind the wrecked coach, a hatless man in ragged trail garb lay sprawled belly-down over a large rock, arms and legs hanging over the rock's blood-washed sides. That would be the jehu, who had no doubt tumbled from the driver's box just before the coach was wrecked.

A man's wretched cry lured Cuno's gaze back to the stage. "No . . . please . . . *noooooo!*"

Cuno couldn't see the poor bastard, but he saw one of the Apache's hunkered down on his knees and making slashing motions with his right arm, performing his devilish knife tricks.

The woman was still screaming. Now she broke loose from several Apaches and ran south, away from the stage. Her torn dress flapped around her waist, leaving her entire white torso bare.

Laughing, two Indians trotted after her. One caught her by her long, golden hair and threw her to the ground. The man ripped off his breechcloth and dove atop her while the other Indian knelt nearby, watching and pounding his thighs with his fists.

Cuno's muscles tensed as he started to rise, intending to run to the woman's aid.

Then he caught himself and squatted back down on his heels. With at least a dozen Indians swarming, there was nothing he could do for her. Nothing he could do for any of them. He'd just started to stand to walk away when movement caught his eye, and he cast his gaze down to the flat again.

A man — or a boy, by the size of him — was crawling out from a sage clump where he'd apparently been thrown when the stage had flipped. The kid glanced over his shoulder at the Indians, most of whom were now focused on the woman, as he crawled on all fours away from the stage. From the halting way he moved, dragging his left leg, he appeared to be injured.

Approaching a cracked boulder and a mesquite tree, he cast another fearful look behind him, then crawled into the crevice between the boulder and the tree, hunkering down where Cuno could see only his head and part of a shoulder.

Behind Cuno, someone kicked a stone. Giving a start, he swung his rifle around, but dropped the barrel when he saw Marcella climbing the rise. Her gun hung low on her thigh, and her hat shaded her face.

"I told you to stay put," he snapped, keeping his voice low.

Ignoring him, Marcella knelt down beside him, peering around the boulder. "What is happening?"

"Apaches ran down a stage."

Below, the blond woman had stopped screaming, and could no longer be seen within the cluster of frenzied Apaches. The one who'd taken her first was walking back to the stage, kicking through the luggage and strewn clothes.

"Apaches run stages down all the time," Marcella said. "There is nothing we can do. Let's go."

She started to stand. Cuno grabbed her arm and cast his gaze back down to where the boy was hiding between the boulder and the mesquite tree.

"There's a kid down there."

She frowned. "So?"

"He's injured, and he's hiding."

"They'll find him soon enough," Marcella

said impatiently. "We must get back after Hudson."

Cuno stared down at the flat, pondering the predicament. True, the Apaches would probably find the kid, but something would not let Cuno abandon him while there was even a slim chance of saving him.

He shook his head. "We wait. When those Apaches are done having their fun down there, they'll leave."

Marcella stared at him, perplexed. She knew it would do no good to argue. When Cuno Massey had made up his mind, there was no changing it. Heaving a frustrated sigh, she leaned back against the rock and folded her arms across her breasts.

She knew it might be a long wait, and it was.

When the Apaches had had their fill of the woman, who gave one final, ear-ringing scream as they killed her, they set the stage on fire and milled around the inferno until the fire had nearly died and the sun had slipped below the desert's rocky rim.

Against a violet sky, Cuno saw their silhouettes gallop away, the hooves pounding crisply in the dusk's hushed silence.

When they'd disappeared in the velvety darkness, Cuno told Marcella again to wait where she was. Hefting his Winchester, he stepped out from behind the rock and started down the knoll, choosing his footing carefully so he would neither fall nor make any noise. He figured all the Indians had left in a group, but he wasn't taking any chances.

When he'd made it to the flat, he paused, looked around the smoldering rubble of the stage, and headed for the boy's hiding place.

"Hey, kid," he said softly when he was about twenty yards away, looking around. "Come on out here — I'm friendly."

Silence.

Cuno cursed as he walked over to the rock and squatted down. All he could see were two wide, staring eyes in the crevice between the rock and the tree. "Come on, damnit!" Cuno reached into the crevice. Finding an arm, he pulled. The boy gave a cry as Cuno jerked him out from his hiding place and pulled him gruffly back toward the knoll.

The boy stumbled silently along on Cuno's heels — a lanky kid in a homespun shirt, cheap string tie, patched broadcloth trousers, and a misshapen slouch hat. Near the base of the knoll, the kid fell, his arm jerking out of Cuno's grasp. The boy clutched his ankle, probably injured during the wreck.

"Come on, blast it," Cuno said, giving the

boy's arm a violent jerk. "We don't have time—"

A guttural shout from behind cut him off. Cuno whipped around, his blood turning to jelly.

Hooves thumped near the stage. A horse whinnied, and brush rustled. Apparently, several Apaches had been lingering near the stage and had heard Cuno and the boy, or had seen them on the knoll.

Hooves pounded. An arrow whistled through the air to Cuno's left, and pinged against a rock.

"Run!" Cuno yelled at the boy, jerking the lad to his feet and giving him a brusque shove from behind.

The boy gave a clipped cry, stumbled, and ran limping up the hill. Cuno dropped to a knee and pumped several rounds at the approaching riders. The rifle leapt in his hands, flashing and barking.

Steadying the barrel with his right hand, he fired two more rounds. He wasn't sure if he hit anything; shooting with his left hand was a cockeyed maneuver. But he thought he heard a yell above the rifle's reports, and about twenty yards below him, the long-haired silhouettes broke their ascent and scattered.

Cuno turned and ran, tripped over a bush,

and fell on his elbows, cursing. Scrambling back to his feet, he overtook the boy, grabbed his arm, and pulled him to the knoll's crest.

Marcella was there, outlined against the sky in which several bright stars were kindling.

"Look out!" she yelled.

Cuno turned to see an Apache on horseback thundering up the knoll, so quickly bridging the gap between them that Cuno could feel the ground shake beneath his boots.

The Apache gave a whoop and drew back the long lance in his hand, the steel blade decorated with tribal feathers glinting in the starlight.

The boy screamed.

Cuno fumbled with his rifle, the blood rushing in his ears as he awaited the spear point he knew was about to impale him.

18

The Apache shrieked savagely before throwing his spear.

Cuno had the rifle to his shoulder, but the butt slipped off his cheek as he tried to steady the barrel with his bandaged right hand. He blinked, his forehead burning, anticipating the lance.

A pistol barked behind him. It barked again.

The Indian grunted as his arm swung forward, launching the feathered spear, which cut through the slack of Cuno's shirt and buried its head in the ground.

By this time, Cuno had steadied the rifle and fired a slug through the Indian's bloody chest as the brave's horse bucked. Arms akimbo, the Apache flew back over his pinto's right rear hip and hit the ground with a grunt.

The horse came down, and Cuno dove

right, avoiding the scissoring hooves. As he scrambled to his knees, he heard Marcella's pistol barking again. Casting his gaze down the knoll, he saw more figures approaching on horseback. Still on his knees and lifting his rifle, he added his own fusillade to Marcella's.

When the Indians had scattered again, he stood and yelled, "Run! *Mooove!*"

The boy was crouched on the ground, frozen with fear.

"Leave him!" Marcella yelled.

Cuno cursed, thrust his rifle at her, and jerked the boy up and over his left shoulder.

"You're an idiot!" Marcella cried as she turned and ran down the other side of the knoll.

Cuno followed her. At the knoll's bottom, Marcella stopped and looked around, confused.

"This way," Cuno said, brushing past her, the boy hanging limply over his shoulder.

Strangely quiet, the kid just hung there as Cuno retraced his footsteps across the desert flats, weaving and stumbling around brush and rocks. Halfway back to the horses, he stopped and shifted the boy from his left shoulder to his right.

"Shh," he told Marcella running up behind him.

She froze and looked around slowly while Cuno listened. The distant clomps and snorts of horses sounded behind them. The Apaches were following slowly, unsure of their course and no doubt wary of an ambush.

"You could not leave well enough alone, could you!" Marcella hissed.

"Shut up," Cuno said, moving out.

He found their mounts five minutes later, standing in a swale with the packhorse. He set the boy on the packhorse and untied the horse from Renegade's tail.

"Let's ride."

Marcella mounted her pinto and lanced Cuno with a heated gaze. "You have probably gotten us killed for some kid we don't even know."

"Yeah, yeah." Cuno gigged Renegade into a trot, heading south, Marcella urging her pinto behind him.

When he'd ridden for twenty minutes, he halted the skewbald paint on a bench near a steep-walled ravine and sat quietly, listening, hearing nothing but the breeze ruffling some mountain scrub along the trail.

Marcella had halted her pinto and was facing him angrily. "The luck of the foolish."

Ignoring her, he kneed Renegade into a trot down the flinty grade.

"We're not out of it yet, but we'll ride till we find a good place to hunker down for the night."

A half hour later, Cuno found a hollow nestled in shrubs with a scarp rising behind it. He helped the boy down against a boulder. Hobbling the horses in a nearby patch of grama grass, he and Marcella silently stripped the tack and packs from their backs, and watered the tired beasts.

With the Apaches about, they didn't even talk about a fire.

Marcella slouched off to the bivouac while Cuno climbed the scarp and listened for horses. When he hadn't heard or seen anything of the Apaches twenty minutes later, he returned to the camp.

Marcella was already asleep in her blankets, curled up on her left side, hat pulled over her cheek to shield her eyes from the starlight. The boy sat against the cracked, egg-shaped rock, legs crossed beneath him, his right ankle swollen.

Cuno set his rifle down and picked up his canteen. He popped the stopper and offered the water to the boy, who accepted it indifferently. He took a sip and paused. Apparently more thirsty than he'd thought, he took several more swallows, lowered the canteen, and ran his hand across his mouth with a sigh. He handed the canteen back to Cuno, who took a long drink, water dribbling down his chin and neck.

"You sure that ankle isn't broken?" he asked, catching his breath. "If it's broken, we should set it."

The boy shook his head.

"What's your name?"

The boy shivered, staring off into the darkness.

"I have to call you something," Cuno said.

For several seconds, the boy said nothing. Then, in a thin voice: "Sandy. Sandy Hilman."

"Your folks on that stage?"

The boy didn't do or say anything for several seconds. Then he nodded dully.

"I'm sorry."

The boy didn't say anything. Cuno knew there was nothing to say.

Cuno grabbed a burlap food sack off his saddle and fished inside for some jerky. He stuck a stick in his mouth and offered the bag to the boy, who ignored it.

Cuno understood. After what he'd been through, he probably wouldn't feel like eating again for days. "Best get some sleep. We'll be up early and riding hard."

He wasn't curious about the boy. Who

Sandy was, where he was going, or where he'd come from meant nothing to Cuno. He'd rescued the boy from the Indians out of some intellectual nod to brotherhood. The feeling was only skin-deep. July's murder had left him without compassion, cold as the stars.

He'd begin looking for Hudson again in the morning. He grabbed his rifle in both hands, grinding the butt into the sand, trying to will the damn sun to rise. . . .

The sun rose only after what seemed like an endless night.

The wind was blowing again, and by ten o'clock Cuno doubted he could have recognized Hudson's trail even if he cut it. Because of the Indians, he didn't dare back-track where he'd left it when he'd rescued the kid.

"Okay," he told the girl, reining his horse to halt on a narrow spur, squinting his eyes against the blowing grit. "Where's Wild Horse Basin?"

Marcella gazed off across a deep canyon falling away on their right. Behind Cuno, the young man sat the packhorse rigidly, his slouch hat pulled low so the wind wouldn't blow it away.

"There . . . it must be there," Marcella

said, pointing across the canyon toward a range of low, blue mountains twenty or thirty miles away.

"You don't know for sure?"

She looked around, her eyes worried and frustrated. "I only crossed this country once, a long time ago," she countered defensively.

She sat her horse regarding him with furrowed brows, holding her hat on her head with one hand, lips set in a pout.

Cuno shook his head disgustedly. "You and the boy wait down in that ravine yonder. I'm gonna take a look around. If I'm not back before dark, sit tight. It might take me a while."

"Where are you going?" she called as he reined his horse away.

"To try to pick up Hudson's trail — where do you think?"

For the next two hours, he angled a quartering trail from east to west. The way this toothy, canyon-scarred country was laid out, he had to drift south for a while, and then north again. But his intention was mainly to drift east to west and hope that if he rode long enough and looked hard enough he'd cut sign.

Around three o'clock that afternoon, blown sand caking his face and his sweat-patched shirt hanging on his muscular trunk, he sawed back on the paint's reins and gave his impassioned gaze to the ground. Four sets of hoof marks shown plainly in the lee of a rocky scarp, angling southwest.

"I'll be goddamned," he said aloud, his heart thumping in his chest.

He whipped his head up when he caught a whiff of wood smoke on the wind. He looked around. To his right was only a boulder-strewn rise, buttery yellow in the sun glare. To his left, a playa white with alkali under a sand-colored curtain of blowing grit stretched to the horizon. Before him was a gently rising sage-and-bear-grass flat stippled with distant buttes.

Another fleeting smoke scent came to his nose on the gyrating wind. It had to be coming from the other side of the slope on his right. Rubbing his chin, Cuno regarded the boulders thoughtfully. He doubted the smoke could be that of the Hudson gang, which he figured had gained another half day on him.

Still, he had to investigate. If the smoke belonged to Apaches, he had to know their exact location and number.

Dismounting, he ground-hitched Renegade back along the trail, in the shade of overhanging rock. Rifle in hand, he found a path twisting around the boulders on the slope. He moved slowly, looking around, disliking how exposed he was on the playa side of the slope.

When he neared the top, he crouched low, jumped onto a flat, sloping boulder, climbed it, and leaned against a stone wall shouldering up on his right. He looked between two more boulders into a narrow, sandy wash on the other side of the butte.

He could smell the smoke better now, as well as the rabbit meat roasting on the fire about thirty yards below, in a shallow pit scooped out of the sand. It was a small fire, the flames wind-battered and torn, the smoke wafting and disappearing nearly as quickly as it rose from the meat skewered on sharpened sticks.

Holding the sticks in a ragged circle around the blaze were three young Apaches.

Two of the red-bronze Indians faced each other, conversing in their guttural tongue. One was gesturing with his hands, as if explaining something the other man was having a hard time absorbing. The third man — a blocky bull of a sun-darkened desert native — was tossing a knife over and over into a nearby chunk of driftwood. The regular, vibrating thuds of the blade skewering the wood rose clearly to Cuno's ears.

Cuno ducked behind a rock. He slid another look around the boulder. The Indians' three horses were hobbled in a thin patch of galleta grass on the other side of the wash, their manes and tails blowing in the wind. There appeared to be just these three Apaches. No women or children, or even any gear except bows and lances piled around a bush. These were warriors on the hoof, probably part of the same gang that had attacked the stage.

Cuno could not rule out the possibility they were looking for him, Marcella, and the boy.

He ducked behind the rock again, squeezing the Winchester's stock with his left hand as troubled thoughts darkened his eyes. He could slip away from the Indians now, and maybe not see them again. Or he might run into them later on, when the upper hand was theirs instead of his. They seemed to be traversing the same country.

He squeezed the rifle's stock harder with his left hand. No use postponing trouble. He'd take them here and now.

He stole another peek at the three Apaches. The chatterbox was on his feet, wheeling in circles and making chopping motions with his right hand. As Cuno watched him kicking sand with his mocassins, he discovered another problem.

The three were too far away for Cuno, with his gimpy hand, to take them all down with the Winchester. He might get one, but he doubted he could get another shell jacked into the chamber before the other two were all over him.

That meant he had to get down close and try to surprise them.

19

Cuno took a minute to ponder his strategy. Finally, he sat down and removed his boots and socks. Rising again, he hefted his rifle and stole another look down the slope.

All three Indians were sitting down now. They'd plucked the stakes from the fire and were hungrily eating the meat.

Cuno had heard stories of the Apaches' acute sense of smell and hearing, and he could only hope the tearing wind, nearly roaring at times, would cover his scent and any noise he might make descending the boulder-littered slope.

Barefoot, he slipped between the two boulders at the slope's crest. The Winchester in his left hand, he jumped down to another rock and crouched behind the one in front of it. Crouching, he cat-footed from rock to rock down the slope, until he found himself bending low behind a flat-topped stone directly behind the three Apaches. He was so close now he could hear them muttering and chewing and sucking marrow from the rabbit bones.

The fire popped and hissed and made gusting sounds when the wind hit it.

Jaws taut, he slipped a careful glance around the boulder. In that quick look he satisfied himself the Indians were still in their same positions around the fire. One had finished eating, however, which meant the other two would be soon.

Cuno had to move quickly. To that end, he quietly jacked a shell in the Winchester's breech. He backed up a couple of steps, then ran forward and sprang atop the flat-topped rock. Smoothly, his face stonily calm, he raised the Winchester to his left shoulder and shot the Apache directly to his right.

As the Indian flew back against the ground, Cuno dropped the rifle from his left hand, palmed his bowie in his injured right, and leapt to the ground before the fire. With a savage thrust of his right leg, he kicked several burning branches at the Indian directly across from him. The Indian had begun standing. Now he turned, yelling and shaking his arms wildly as flames leapt at his buckskin breeches, scorching the leather and

248

basting his ankles. Cuno whipped his right hand up, throwing his bowie end over end, the blade disappearing to the hilt in the Apache's belly.

Before Cuno could turn to the last Apache, the beefy savage was on top of him — all slippery, smelly, two-hundred-plus pounds of him. He drove Cuno sideways to the ground. Brain-fogging pain lanced Cuno's shoulder and spread through his chest and into his ribs.

Kneeling on top of Cuno, the Indian reached for the knife on his belt. Before he could get it out, Cuno shoved upward with all his strength, giving a soul-shuddering yell. The Indian rolled to the left, and Cuno thrust himself to his feet.

In his mind, these men became the men who had killed July. His face became a snarling mask of rage. The rage made his head and limbs light and dulled the pain in his right hand.

As the Apache climbed to his feet, Cuno dove on top of him, throwing him back down. He punched the Indian several times in the face. Then the Indian kneed Cuno off, chopped him savagely with his left hand. Cuno reeled on his knees, the world spinning, but when the Indian jumped at him again, he was ready, rising, pivoting to his left. He buried his bandaged right hand deep in the savage's belly.

The hand seared with pain, but Cuno hardly noticed. The Apache looked stunned. He was only fighting an intruder in his ancestral territory. Cuno wasn't fighting one man. He was fighting his father's killer, and he was fighting Page Hudson, and he was fighting the very Creator who had made it possible for Cuno to lose his beautiful young wife, the last person on earth he loved with all his being.

He wasn't sure how long he'd had the Indian down beneath him and had been pummeling the Apache's head with a heavy rock before he froze, holding the rock aloft. Wild-eyed, he stared down at the Apache.

Somehow, he'd gotten the man's calico bandanna down around his neck. He was holding the ends with his left hand, and using them to jerk the Indian's head up as he'd brought the stone down to meet it. There wasn't much left of the Indian's head now. The right temple was caved in like a watermelon, matting the hair and entire face with blood and white flecks of brain matter. The Indian's trunk hung slack in Cuno's hand.

Cuno released the bandanna. The Indian's head dropped with a soft thud in the sand.

Heaving off his knees, his chest rising and falling heavily, Cuno stood. He looked down at the dead Indian, and then at the other two lying about the fire. The wood he'd kicked from the fire lay strewn, pale orange flames licking at it between wind gusts.

Cuno retrieved his knife, slipped it into his scabbard, and moved toward the slope. His feet were heavy. Suddenly, he became aware of his throbbing right hand, and looked down at it. It hung at his side, the bandage gone, awash in blood.

Ignoring it, he started up the slope toward his horse.

In the ravine where Cuno had left her and the boy, Marcella sat on a small ledge shelving out from the rock behind her, and brought her cigarette to her lips. Dully, she regarded the boy sitting several feet away, looking off down the canyon, his own face expressionless, the ceaseless wind working at his short, brown hair shaved high above his ears.

She didn't blame the boy for the delay, nor for luring the Indians onto their trail. She blamed Cuno. He was the one who'd wanted to save the boy from the Apaches. Still, she could not help regarding the kid with mute scorn as she smoked, shaking her head, then sliding her gaze around the sun-seared ridges towering around them.

To make herself feel better, she tried to think about what she would do with the money when she found it. A fancy brothel in San Francisco? Maybe a saloon with a dozen stylish bartenders and several private gambling salons . . .

Interrupting her reverie, a light flashed in the corner of her vision.

She turned her head left, shaded her eyes with a hand. On a distant, southern pinnacle, the light flashed again, as though off a belt buckle or a spur. Squinting her eyes, she saw a man-shaped shadow flit amongst the rocks and disappear.

Lifting her hand again to her eyes, Marcella stood and stared. A man was out there, a single rider. Could it be Cuno?

She studied the place in the ridge where the rider had disappeared for several minutes, the boy watching her as he squinted against the sun glare.

If the rider had been Cuno, he'd been riding in the wrong direction — away from her. Marcella's pulse quickened. There were only two reasons he would do that. One, he was lost. Two, he had found Hudson's tracks and was more determined to run the gang to ground than to return for her and the boy.

The second possibility weighed on her heavily. She wheeled for the horses. To the boy she said, "Come on if you're coming with me." Although she resented his presence, she couldn't leave him — mostly because she was afraid of what Cuno might do to her if she did.

Five minutes later, Marcella gigged her pinto up the crumbling path from the canyon, trailing the boy on the packhorse, his thin legs draped over the panniers. His face held little expression but for a faint wariness under the shading brim of his slouch hat.

Marcella led the procession along the canyon's rim, then down into a swale rimmed with smoky scrub oaks and greasewood. On the other side, she found a path littered with mountain-goat scat. She followed its serpentine route for at least two miles before she came to the spot where she thought the man had been.

She dismounted and looked around. Bending over, folding her hair back from her face with both hands, she cursed softly. She squatted down and cuffed her hat back from her head, studying the overlaid tracks of four horses.

Straightening, she cursed in Spanish. Her heart pounded and her knees warmed with anxiety and anticipation.

"What is it?" the boy asked her.

"Never mind," she said, poking her boot through a stirrup and swinging atop the pinto, which, sensing its rider's agitation, shook its head and blew.

The horse jerked forward with a whinny. Drawing back on the reins, Marcella looked around.

Should she ride back where she'd come from or straight ahead, in the direction Page Hudson's gang had gone?

Hudson was near. She was no tracker, but she could see plain as salt that those tracks were fresh.

Not sure what she would do once she caught up with Hudson, but not wanting to lose him again, she gigged her horse along the tracks. Wordlessly, the boy shadowed her on the packhorse, but she was no longer aware of him.

Hudson was near, which meant the map was near. She shivered. She might be only a day's ride from the gold.

Her pinto was clomping along an ancient riverbed when she saw something move in a jumble of mushroom-shaped rocks ahead. Before she could halt the horse, she saw movement in the corner of her right eye — a shadow flying at her from another natural cairn.

The man plunged into her, knocking her off her horse. With a scream, she hit the ground hard. She rolled several feet, the man rolling with her, first on top of her, then beneath, then on top again. When she'd finally stopped rolling and was gasping air into her battered lungs, she found herself staring up into the scarred, grinning countenance of Page Hudson.

"Marcella Jiminez," Hudson said with open surprise. "What in the hell are you doin' here?"

"Get off me, pig!" she cried, gaining a shallow breath. She tried to punch Hudson, but she could get no power behind her fist. He easily grabbed it and pressed it to the ground. Pinning both her arms to her sides, he stared down at her, his face a mask of incredulity.

"Goddamn hellcat!"

She kicked at him. Unable to reach him with her legs, she resorted to cursing and spitting. It only inflamed him. Straddling her on his knees, he slapped her face several times with both his gloved hands. The flurry of brain-rattling licks left her reeling in a fog, sobbing, her eyes fluttering.

A horse whinnied and stomped to Hudson's right. He turned to see the packhorse the kid was riding bucking and fiddle-footing, quartering around until the boy flopped off the dun's right hip and hit the ground with a grunt. The horse ran bucking back the way it had come, in the dust blowing behind Marcella's retreating pinto.

Hudson grabbed Marcella's revolver from her holster. Straightening, he saw his three compatriots moving out from the rocks around the trail, rifles in their hands.

"Grab the kid," he told Billy Saber, jerking his head at the boy, who'd pushed himself up on his hands and knees and looked as though he were thinking about making a run for it.

Saber got to the kid just as the boy had climbed to his feet. Casually, Saber jabbed his rifle butt against the back of the kid's head. The boy gave a cry as he flew forward and hit the ground on his face. He tried pushing himself up again, and passed out.

"How's that?" Saber said, grinning.

"It'll do," Hudson said, turning his scowl back to Marcella. He knelt over her, staring down with acrimony plain in his slitted eyes. "Now then, sugarplum, just what in the hell are you doin' out here?"

Marcella swallowed and looked up at him through the spray of dusty hair in her face. Her brain was numb and her ears were ringing. She felt as though someone were holding a hot iron to each cheek. She'd heard Hudson's question, but was not sure how to answer.

The sudden flicker of understanding in Hudson's eyes told her she didn't have to.

Hudson laughed dubiously. "You followed me all the way out here for the map." He shook his head and scrubbed his face with his hand. "Good Lord, girl, you're even crazier than I am!"

Hudson laughed again.

"Who's the kid?" Clevis O'Malley asked. He and the other two men stood around, casting long shadows.

"What I wanna know," Hudson said, "is who else is out here." He ran a cautious gaze around the rocks along the trail, craned a look back north where the two horses had disappeared.

"What do you mean?" Kenny Wilks asked.

He had a bloody bandage around his head. Yesterday, they'd run into more Apaches, and he'd been grazed by a war lance. They'd lost their horses and spent the last several hours running them down.

Hudson looked at O'Malley. "When you spied these two behind us, you didn't see anyone else?"

Clevis shrugged his heavy shoulders and shook his shaggy head. "Nope."

Turning his gaze back to Marcella, he swung his arm back and down, smacking her hard with the back of his right hand. The blow turned her head sideways and raised another red welt on her cheek.

"Who else is out here?"

She turned her hate-filled eyes on him, but said nothing. Page Hudson was a savage. He would kill her without a thought. Cuno Massey was her only hope of survival now.

Hudson smacked her again.

"I know there's someone out here with you, girl. You didn't make it through these Injun-infested badlands all by yourself. Who and how many? Tell me or so help me I'll beat your head to a bloody goddamn pulp!"

With that, he smacked her again. Marcella screamed and cursed, then tightened her jaws until they ran in a straight line to her chin. "There is no one! I came alone for the gold!"

"Horseshit!" Hudson barked, and brought the back of his right hand against her red-mottled face. "You're stupid, bitch, but you ain't stupid enough to think you could fight off the whole damn Apache nation *and* kill me for the map!" His voice grew even more threatening as he ground the angry phrases through gritted teeth. "Tell me who's out here, Marcella. . . ."

She stared up at him defiantly, her ears ringing so loudly she could barely hear him anymore above the unrelenting wind.

"All right," he said with a fateful air, "you asked for it."

Drawing his ten-inch bowie from his belt scabbard with one hand, he ripped her shirt off her shoulder with the other. With another thrust, the shirt tore away from her bosom, exposing her olive breasts.

Hudson lowered the razor-sharp, glinting knife blade. Her heaving breasts rippled with gooseflesh.

Marcella screamed.

20

When he returned to his horse, Cuno rewrapped his hand, then mounted up and rode back toward the ravine, intending to retrieve Marcella and the boy and get back after the Hudson gang. Reining Renegade to a halt on the ravine's ridge, he cast his gaze below, his forehead instantly furrowing.

Marcella and the boy were nowhere in sight. The only sign of them was a few fresh horse apples, two cigarette butts, and a scattering of foot- and hoofprints.

Dismounting and stepping onto a rock jutting out over the canyon, reins in hand, Cuno called Marcella's name. If they were still in the area, he doubted they'd have strayed very far from where he'd left them.

The only reply was the wind funneling through the hollow and swirling dust up along its banks.

"Crazy damn girl," Cuno said under his

breath. She must have gotten impatient and gone after him, or after the gold.

Mumbling oaths, he dropped Renegade's reins and descended the sloping bank into the ravine. It didn't take him long to spy the tracks Marcella and the boy had made when they'd mounted up and left. Returning to Renegade, Cuno swung up into the saddle and followed the tracks southwest, skirting the rim of the ravine for a hundred yards. Then he swung straight south, traced a meandering path west around a mesa, and headed south again, trailing an ancient riverbed.

The wind was relentless, scouring his face and eyes with grit. His eyes burned and watered, and he had to dab at them frequently with a corner of his neckerchief. He kept his hat pulled down low to keep it from blowing off his head. Occasionally, the wind obliterated the prints he was following, but he managed to pick up traces again as he rode farther.

The sky was nearly the same color as the surrounding terrain, so that the whole world was the sickly red of an underripe tomato. The sand in the air was so thick that at times he could see barely thirty feet in front of him.

He'd ridden for a quarter hour when he

held up short, his eyes on the ground. The two sets of horse prints he'd been following suddenly turned back upon themselves. The lengths of the strides told Cuno the horses had galloped back the way they'd come, then sharply angled off to the west, through a scattering of dead oaks growing along a bone-dry seep.

Gigging his horse ahead, Cuno soon came to the place — a narrowing of the riverbed between piles of balloon-shaped rock — where the horses had halted and spun around. Men's boot prints converged on the trail. Broad scuff marks in the sand betrayed a struggle.

Holding his hat brim down over his forehead, Cuno looked around at the rocks. Four men had intercepted Marcella and the boy. It would be too damn much of a coincidence if those four men were not Hudson and his compadres. Yet it didn't make sense. The men were well off the trace Cuno had picked up after first leaving the ravine. Something had turned them south and east.

His heart fluttering eagerly, he picked through the mess of tracks in the area. A quarter hour later, he was following five sets of hoofprints. Hudson's gang, as well as Marcella and the boy, were all mounted on five horses, heading more or less south.

After what he figured to be about five plodding miles, he gave Renegade's bridle reins a backward twitch. It didn't take much to halt the skewbald paint in this weather. Before Cuno, a sage-peppered bowl yawned wide, abutted on the south and east sides by low, craggy mountains.

In the middle of the hollow was a town. At times, because of the blowing dust, Cuno could barely see the settlement. It wasn't much — a motley collection of tin-roofed shacks standing in no particular order amidst the sage and dun-colored mounds, stretching not more than a quarter mile from east to west. Five sets of hoofprints, barely visible, stretched off through the sage, heading right for it.

Blinking his eyes against the grit, Cuno sat his mount, staring through the howling dust at the abandoned town.

"Welcome to Wild Horse," he said, the words a raspy whisper lost in the wind.

An hour earlier, Hudson, his companions, Marcella, and the boy had entered the ghost town of Wild Horse through the east end, passing the church on their left and a mercantile on their right — hollow frame buildings tilting against the wind, the paint blistered and peeling, tumbleweeds piled around them like sandbags against a flood. A dray and a Conestoga missing its wheels sat abandoned along the street. Otherwise, the main drag was a wide, empty alley scalloped with blown sand with here and there a Spanish bayonet.

The big, faded sign hanging over the mercantile's loading dock boasted professional mining supplies and tough denim trousers — "none tougher in the Southwest!" The cracked red sign screeched as the wind swung it madly and pelted it with dirt.

The gang passed several more stores standing with good-sized gaps between them in which sand had mounded and the sage grew sparsely. Trash had been thrown there, and rusty tin cans now clattered down the silent main street, which still bore the ruts of ore wagons.

Hudson stared at all the glass panes in the windows he passed. When the town had gone bust only two and a half years ago, the veins paying out virtually all at once, the townsfolk must have left in such a hurry they didn't even bother to take the glass, an expensive commodity this far off the beaten path.

He gave his attention to the four saloons, two on each side of the street. Two signs were so faded he couldn't make out the names, and the sign of one had blown down entirely, punching a hole through the porch roof.

"This place gives me the creeps," Kenny Wilks said, glancing around like he expected ghouls to dash out at him from one of the empty businesses.

"I have to agree with the younker," Clevis O'Malley said above the howling wind. "Now I know why they call 'em ghost towns."

Billy Saber chuckled. "You chickenshits!"

Ignoring the others, Hudson reined his horse up at the building with a doctor's office occupying a lean-to off its east side. Staring up at the faded lettering on the facade, just above the second-story balcony, he squinted his eyes against the grit.

"What you lookin' for, Page?" O'Malley yelled above the wind.

"The Lost Lady Saloon," Hudson yelled back. As several of the large, scrolled letters revealed themselves between wind gusts, he added with a tight smile, "And I think I found it right here."

"This where your brother hid the gold?" Kenny Wilks asked. He was leading the horse carrying the Mexican girl and the boy, both of whose feet were tied beneath the belly of their mount, their wrists lashed together before them. They both had their heads bowed against the wind.

"That's right," Hudson said, swinging down from his horse. "Leave it to old Rick to hide loot in a saloon." He chuckled as he tossed his reins up to Billy Saber. "Billy, stable the horses somewhere. Give 'em oats and plenty of water. Tomorrow, my man, they'll be haulin' gold!"

Hudson used his bowie to cut the ropes tying Marcella and the boy's ankles. He grabbed each by an arm and pulled them off the pinto, both falling with startled cries, hitting the sandy ground with grunts. The girl cursed and spit sand from her mouth.

"You are a worthless pig!" she shouted above the wind, scrambling onto her butt.

Hudson grinned and thrust his hips at her. He tossed the barb's reins to Saber, who rode off down the street trailing all four horses. Then he yanked Marcella to her feet. "Get in there!" he ordered, kicking her backside. She screamed and bolted onto the boardwalk, tripping and falling on her hands and knees.

Behind Hudson, O'Malley pulled Sandy up by his hair and gave him a kick similar to the kick Hudson had given Marcella. The boy tripped over the girl, going down with a cry.

Hudson stepped over them, opened the unlocked saloon door, pulled the boy up by the hair again, and threw him through the door. Marcella was crawling onto her hands. Hudson grabbed her by the hair, and threw her in after the boy.

She screamed as she stumbled forward, then rattled off another string of epithets hot enough to melt a snowbank.

Billy Saber snickered. "Page, I think she just called you queer."

"I say we kill that little bitch," Clevis O'Malley barked as he followed Hudson through the door. "She's rawhidin' my balls but good."

"Not before I get a piece of her," Kenny Wilks said. "She might be loud, but I bet she bucks good. . . ."

"Keep that donkey dick in your pants, Kenny," Hudson ordered. "No one gets her before I do. And don't kill her, Cleve. Massey's apt to tread a little lighter if he knows we have her and the boy."

"What makes you think he gives a shit, Page?" Wilks asked. He'd entered the saloon behind Hudson and O'Malley, slapping his hat against his thigh, and shut the door behind him. "I mean, to have followed us this far, he's gotta be plumb kill-crazy nuts!"

Hudson was looking around the saloon,

fists on his hips, as though he were appraising the decor. "Yeah, but it looks like he's a kill-crazy nut with a soft spot for women and children."

When he'd threatened to carve her up with his bowie knife, Marcella had told Hudson about how Cuno had rescued the boy, and that she and Cuno had trailed Hudson from Bella Lord's.

"Imagine bein' so torn up over one dead woman that you trail the likes of us through a hundred miles of badlands," Kenny Wilks said with an air of grave bewilderment. He shook his head. "I just don't get it. I mean, doesn't he know how many women there are on this earth?"

Hudson was no longer listening. He had his map out and was studying it, frowning. Then he turned his gaze around the dusty, cobwebbed saloon with its few scattered tables coated with mice droppings. A heavy layer of dun-colored dust covered the counter, and the mirror behind it was so dusty it no longer reflected. Part of the upstairs balcony railing had crumbled onto the main floor, and Hudson stepped over it as he read his map and walked toward the room's rear. He stepped behind the bar and circled back toward the front of the room, running a gloved hand along the counter, causing an avalanche of dust. As he passed, he read his map and counted his footsteps.

Marcella sat on the floor where Hudson had thrown her, head down, matted hair hanging in her eyes — the picture of dejection. The boy lay nearby, facedown on the floor, fists up near his shoulders. His head was turned toward the bar, his eyes watching Hudson with a strange mix of curiosity and fear.

O'Malley and Wilks watched Hudson too, their own expressions behind their dust-masked faces betraying anxious hope.

"You . . . you findin' it, Page?" Wilks asked with quiet desperation.

"Shut up," Hudson said, holding the map up to the wan light filtering through the windows. "I'm tryin' to read Rick's scrawl here at the bottom."

Hudson studied the paper for several more seconds. Then he looked behind him. Turning, he set the map on the bar and walked several paces toward the rear of the room.

He stopped, a look of grave concentration smoothing the angular lines of his unshaven face. He jerked slightly as he tapped a foot on the floor. He tapped the foot in several places. When he found the hollow sound he'd been listening for, he bent down and grew silent.

Finally, he straightened and thrust his sand-colored face across the bar. "Clevis, find me somethin' to pry these floorboards up."

The big Irishman scowled and threw his meaty arms out from his sides. "Where the hell am I gonna find somethin' like that?"

"This was a mining town, weren't it?" Hudson said. "Find me a pick!"

"All right," O'Malley muttered, glancing warily around, reluctant to wander out alone in this eerie little graveyard of a town. "I'll look for a damn pick. . . ."

Finally, hitching up his pants and snugging his hat down on his head, he left. Ten minutes later, he returned, flushed with anxiety and wielding a rusty pick with a splintered handle.

"What took you so damn long?" Hudson complained as O'Malley handed the pick across the bar.

"Just 'cause it's a mining town, don't mean they had picks growing outta the cactus. Found this one here half-buried in an alley. Dead man in that alley too," the big man added. "A skeleton wearing a full set of clothes, two bullets holes in his shirt!"

With an impatient chuff, Hudson grabbed

the pick and crouched behind the bar. O'Malley and Wilks stood watching expectantly.

The boy remained in his same prone position on the floor. Marcella had scooted back against a wood stove and was staring darkly at the bar, from behind which thuds and taps issued.

"Y-you need any help, Page?" Kenny Wilks asked after several minutes.

The only response was the screech of a pried floorboard. The screeching and pounding peppered with Hudson's grunts and groans continued for several minutes. Then suddenly there was silence, made heavier by the sound of the keening wind and the sand pelting the walls and windows.

Hudson whistled.

"What is it?" O'Malley asked with an eager glint in his eyes.

Behind the bar, Hudson straightened, a wide, shit-eating grin stretching his sand-flecked, unshaven face. With a flourish he set upon the bar top one shining, golden bar, dust puffing off the mahogany around it.

"Clevis, my boy, it is my scoundrel brother Rick's legendary gold!"

"Holy shit!" Wilks tittered, clapping his hands together and eagerly wringing them.

Tearing his eyes from the gold, Hudson

smiled at Kenny. Then the smile transformed to a gaping frown. He thrust an arm out, pointing at something behind Wilks.

"Look out, Kenny! *Grab her!*"

21

Kenny turned just as the girl, who had cat-footed across the floor, grabbed his .45 from his holster with both hands and thumbed the hammer back. The gun exploded as Marcella grabbed it, thrusting up. The bullet plunked into a rafter, felling a mouse nest and splinters.

"Jackals!" the girl screamed. "I'll kill . . . *you!*" With that, she gave another jerk, and the gun exploded again, this time plugging the mirror behind the bar and causing Hudson to duck.

"Clevis, grab her, damnit!" he shouted.

O'Malley was moving toward her and Wilks as they turned a bizarre dance around the wood stove, their arms raised above their heads, wrestling for the gun. The pistol barked again, checking O'Malley's progress as the big Irishman dropped down behind a table, yelling, "Kenny, get it away from her!"

"That's what I'm trying to do!" Wilks shouted back in a pinched voice, turning again, trying to wrench the gun from the girl's surprisingly strong grip. The gun coughed two more times before O'Malley made a dive for Marcella, throwing her to the floor, pinning her under his two-hundred-plus pounds as Kenny at last jerked the smoking revolver from her hand.

Marcella screamed angrily and pounded O'Malley with her fists.

"Clevis, hog-tie that bitch!" Hudson ordered, his voice cracking with anticipation.

"Kenny!" Clevis yelled as he deflected the shrieking girl's fists. "Rope!"

Wilks dashed outside and retrieved the rope they'd used to lash her to her horse. By the time he and O'Malley had her tied to a chair, she'd spent herself. She slumped in the chair, shoulders rounded, sobbing, looking half-savage with her badly mussed hair hanging about her face and falling in dust-caked tangles down her back. Earlier, Hudson had torn several buttons from her shirt. The garment hung open now, revealing a good portion of her breasts, attracting several flat, lusty gazes.

While Wilks and O'Malley dealt with the girl, Hudson had been piling the gold bars on the mahogany. Both men turned now, their knees nearly buckling under the weighty thrill of all that gold — four gold bars piled atop the mahogany and nearly filling the long, narrow room with their spectacular golden glow.

The door rattled, and Billy Saber appeared. "Well, I'll be damned," he said. He cuffed his hat back off his forehead and stood grinning, fists on his hips. "It wasn't no wild-goose chase after all!"

"That's it," Hudson said as he placed a fifth gold bar atop the two-tiered stack. "Five gold bars. That's roughly twenty-five thousand dollars. Enough for us to retire in Old Mexico for at least ten years."

The men studied the bars with silent admiration for several minutes, as though in a daze. O'Malley picked one up, caressed it like a speckled pup, then gently set it back upon the stack. "Now, that's a purty picture!" He frowned with sudden concern and jerked a thumb over his shoulder.

"What about them?" he said, meaning Marcella and the boy.

"Yeah," Saber said. "I still don't understand why we didn't kill 'em when we first found 'em" — the lines in his horsey face smoothed and his eyes blazed — "after we took our pleasure from the Mescin."

Hudson stood behind the gold, both

hands on the bar, like a bartender admiring his best concoction yet. "You idiots leave her alone. She's my bodyguard, damn ye."

"I say we leave her and the twirp and ride on outta here," Kenny Wilks said. He was sitting in a backless chair, and he was fussing with the bandage on his head. The girl had reopened the wound, and he was worrying about infection again.

"Not in this sandstorm." Hudson walked out from behind the bar. He came down the outside of the counter and moseyed up to the gold like a priest to a rack of candles. "Besides, our horses are tired. We'll sit right here tonight, take care of Massey when he comes, and head for Mexico in the mornin'. I'm bettin' the storm will blow itself out by first light."

"These two are just too damn much trouble, Page," O'Malley growled, shaking his head and staring at the boy. Sandy Hilman sat half under a table, staring back at O'Malley with open worry in his eyes.

"Shut up, Clevis, and leave those two alone." Hudson stared at the gold. Twenty-five thousand dollars. And it would all be his once he'd ridden himself of these three knob-headed peckerwoods.

"Tie the kid to Marcella," Hudson said woodenly. "Back-to-back in front of the door."

Hudson would kill the kid when he killed the others, after Massey was finally off his trail. As for Marcella, Hudson could get a pretty price for her down in Old Mexico.

Besides, it was still a long ride to the border, and a man had certain needs only a woman could fulfill. . . .

When Marcella and the boy had been tied back-to-back just inside the saloon door, Hudson ordered O'Malley and Saber outside to keep watch for Massey. "Find a high place and keep your eyes open," he ordered the men as, complaining, they headed out the door into the blast of wind and sand. "No sleepin' till Massey's dead!" he yelled as Saber drew the door closed behind him.

"What do you want me to do, Page?" Wilks asked. He was staring at the gold on the bar eagerly and probing the bloody spot on his bandage with his fingers.

"Guard the back door from the alley."

Wilks gaped. "From outside?"

"You heard me, you goddamn sissy. Get out there!"

Wilks was about to argue, but then he saw the cold, hard look in Hudson's eyes. With a sigh, he got up, strode through a door at the room's rear, and disappeared into a storage room. Another door was thrown open with a muffled wind blast. Wilks slammed it so hard the floor jumped.

Hudson slacked into a chair and began rolling a smoke. He leaned down and mugged for the girl, bugging his eyes out, taunting her. "Ah . . . just look at all that gold. So close and yet so *far!*"

Marcella turned her face to him, spit, and turned away.

Hudson wiped her hot saliva off his cheek with his hand, wrinkling his nose, his eyes flattening with menace.

Cuno lounged in a nest of cracked rocks and greasewood, his rifle in his hand, feet propped before him. He watched the night close slowly over the windblown, dust-veiled town sitting in a lumpy, brushy desert swale a half mile away. He'd watered Renegade and ground-hitched the horse in a depression behind him, and now he sat, chewing a weed while he stared at the town.

Hudson's boys would be waiting for him. There was no doubt about that. But he wasn't in any hurry. He doubted they'd go anywhere in this storm.

He waited through the long night, listening to the wind howl, hunkering into his raised shirt collar and wincing against the grit thrown into the rocks. Around three, impatience chewed at him, tingled in his fingers and feet, but he made himself relax. At four-thirty by his pocket watch, he retrieved Renegade and began following a shallow wash toward the town.

In the saloon, Marcella and the boy slept fitfully, arms behind their backs, heads canted forward over their chests. Occasionally the boy woke moaning from a dream, lifted his head, glanced around the lantern-lit room, then drifted back to sleep.

Hudson smoked and drank coffee he'd perked on the wood stove, having found several lengths of mesquite in the back room. He paced, staying clear of the windows, listening for gun reports above the anxious wind.

Massey would come. Hudson knew it. And Massey knew Hudson knew it. Rankled, Hudson chewed his quirley and sidled up to the big front window right of the door, looking out.

Yeah, the son of a bitch knew he knew it, and loved every minute of Hudson's knowing . . . and squirming.

"Should've killed the son of a bitch back in Krantzburg, when we had the chance." But who would have guessed the kid would be this pesky? For lordy sakes, they'd only killed his *woman,* and as Billy Saber had pointed out, there were more fish in the sea!

Seeing little but a shunting darkness and occasional gusts of grit, Hudson turned away from the window. Behind the bar he found playing cards. He sat at a table, cursed softly, and began laying out a game of solitaire.

Outside the saloon's rear door, Kenny Wilks huddled in the alley, between two stacks of rotten shipping crates, facing the main street. He'd lifted his collar against the wind, sitting with his knees up, his rifle poking up between them. He gritted his teeth and watched for moving shadows in the howling darkness, occasionally slapping his own cheeks when he grew fatigued. If Hudson caught him sleeping, he'd probably cut his throat to spare a bullet.

East of him, Clevis O'Malley stood in the church's bell tower, his rifle cradled in his arms. The big man's eyes were wide as he watched the murky darkness below, through which he could barely make out the lines and angles of other buildings. He could hear nothing but the steady rush and keening of the wind.

He came to one edge of the bell tower, leaned out to look over the side, then straightened. Fatigue washing over him, he yawned wide, stretched the kinks out of his neck, then turned and walked to the other side of the tower. He had to keep moving or fall asleep.

On the west edge of town, Billy Saber sat between the two open doors of the livery barn's loft, feet hanging over the outside wall. His shotgun lay across his lap. Cupping the coal in his palm, he brought his quirley to his lips and nudged the boredom aside with thoughts of the girl, remembering the sway of her full breasts in her torn shirt.

He'd been without a woman now for several days, and he imagined the good time he'd have with her when Massey was dead and they could relax. Hudson could go to hell.

Saber knew Hudson had no intention of sharing the gold. He'd read it in the gang leader's deep-set eyes. That was all right with Saber. He had no intention of sharing the gold with anyone either. As soon as Massey was dead, Saber's compatriots would be dead as well.

Saber's eyes narrowed as he drew deep on the stubby cigarette, the coal glowing brightly against his palm. Soon the gold and the girl would be his alone.

The wiry firebrand crushed out the cigarette on the loft floor and stared across the desert cloaked by the wavering curtain of grit. The air had a metallic odor mixed with the smell of creosote and sun-scorched sand. Saber blinked angrily and scowled.

Where was that son of a bitch anyway? Why didn't he show?

To calm his nerves, he returned his thoughts to the girl. His blood warmed as he remembered that torn shirt, those slender, exposed shoulders, those hanging breasts, nipples jutting through the filthy cloth. He'd have a hell of time with her in the morning!

When he was finished with her, he'd kill her. Nothing worse than the same girl twice, and knowing her, she'd track him for the gold.

Suddenly, he jerked his head left. Between wind gusts, he'd seen something move near the adobe shack sitting across the street from the livery's corral. His heart picking up its beat, Saber stood slowly, moved behind the wall, and stared out, squeezing his rifle hungrily.

Massey. It had to be.

It wouldn't be long now, Saber thought, the girl and the gold flashing once more in his mind.

22

Cuno ground-hitched Renegade north of Wild Horse and entered the town from the northwest. From an alley, he saw the light in the saloon window. The light could be a trap. Best to scour the town before approaching the saloon, he thought.

He was creeping along the north edge of the town, amidst the abandoned shacks and cactus, when he spied a man-shaped shadow between the livery barn's open doors. He slipped back behind the crumbling adobe house and, gripping his rifle before him, moved slowly west along the shack's rear wall.

One or two men might be in the saloon, but he doubted they all were. Hudson would have posted someone among the vacant buildings, no doubt with orders to shoot anything that moved.

Swinging his gaze behind him, he saw a

faint pale flush in the eastern sky. The wind had diminished slightly, but the grit still blew with a vengeance — tiny javelins pricking his skin. That was all right. This morning, the sound-covering wind was his ally.

At the shack's northwestern corner, he stopped. He could not see the livery barn from this angle. About a hundred feet before him, the wash he'd followed into town curved around the shack, snaking southward. Forming a plan, he bolted out from behind the shack, ran crouching, and dropped into the wash with a grunt.

The wash was only a few feet deep. He dropped to his belly and stole a peek over the lip, gazing across the rocks and cactus at the livery barn. Through the swirling sand, the building was little more than a smudge, the open doors a darker stain within the smudge. Cuno could hear the wind creaking the timbers.

He could not see the man he'd seen before, but he bet the man had seen him.

He slid back to the bottom of the wash and crawled south on all fours. There was enough light that he could avoid the prickly pear and ocotillo, but crawling with the rifle in his one good hand was awkward and slow.

When he'd crawled twenty-five yards, the

wash deepened, the defile narrowing. He stood and walked slowly, crouching to keep his head below the lip, looking around.

Most likely the man from the livery wouldn't waste time summoning the others. The town was small enough that, without the wind, he could have yelled for his compatriots. But the wind was still howling loudly enough that his voice would have been lost.

Seeing little but blowing sand, Cuno moved farther down the wash. He stepped around a bend, gripping his rifle in both hands. Ahead rose a sound like a tin can. Cuno jacked a shell and crouched, peering into the blowing grit.

Something moved. Cuno raised the rifle, froze.

A coyote stood looking at him over a trash heap at the bottom of the wash. Suddenly, the coyote wheeled, trotted off with its tail down, leapt up the ridge in two bounds, and disappeared.

Cuno lowered the rifle and scowled into the grit.

On the livery barn's bottom floor, Saber crouched and stared out at the wash, little more than a gray shadow snaking around the town's western edge. He'd seen the shadow steal out from behind the shack and dash into the wash.

An eager sneer curling his lip, he ran crouching across the main drag and sidled up to the shack's front wall. Broken glass crunching silently beneath his boots, he moved slowly toward the ravine, watching, swinging his gaze from left to right, steeling himself.

Several feet from the wash's lip, he lunged forward and raised his gun. He saw a good chunk of the shallow wash from this point, and Massey was not here. Seeing the scuffed trough where a man had crawled southward, he followed it, squinting against the blowing sand, keeping one eye on the sign at the bottom of the eroded wash and one on the banks rising sharply around him.

As he moved cautiously, one step at a time, swinging his head slowly from left to right, Saber felt a prickling under his collar. His heart beat a persistent rhythm against his breastbone. It was not fear but excitement, the hunger for the kill he'd known since he'd shot his first man in Tie Siding, Wyoming, thirteen years ago.

He swung a look behind him. Seeing no one, he continued down the wash, which made a slow left curve around the town's southern edge.

Unbeknownst to Saber, Cuno Massey stole out from behind a large cottonwood and a sapling on the wash's southwestern rim. He ran up along the rim on the balls of his feet, trying to make as little noise as possible. When he was nearly parallel with Saber, Saber became aware of someone behind him and began turning.

Cuno dropped his rifle and sprang off the rim.

He plunged into Saber as the killer, wide-eyed with shock, began lifting his shotgun. Cuno knocked the gun away with his left arm and drove Saber to the ground. Saber gave a grunt as he landed in a tuft of sage and jagged rocks. Quickly, Cuno scooted onto his knees and brought his right fist sharply against Saber's face, the smack of knuckles against bone barely audible above the keening wind.

As Cuno was about to bring the fist forward again, Saber bucked powerfully. Cuno fell to Saber's left, hitting the ground on a shoulder and rolling onto his back. He'd started up again when Saber landed a hard left on his cheek.

Cuno's head flew back, his eyes fluttering. When his vision cleared, he saw a revolver in Saber's right hand.

The hard case was grinning as he ratcheted the hammer back and jabbed the gun at Cuno's mouth. "Open wide, you son of a *bitch!*"

The last word was voiced not with venom, but on a sudden burst of air exploding from his lungs. Saber jerked forward, glancing down at the bowie Cuno had just poked through his belly button and buried to the hide-wrapped hilt in Saber's blood-soaked shirt.

Cuno easily grabbed the gun from Saber's sagging hand and heaved the killer aside. Saber rolled onto his back with a sigh, grunting and cursing and trying futilely to hold his belly together.

"Bastard," he rasped through blood-frothy lips.

Cuno stared down at him, his face a stony mask. "For my wife."

He brought his left arm back, then swung it down and back, connecting soundly with Saber's jaw. The back of the hard case's head smacked the ground hard, bouncing, his fluttering eyes rolling back in his head.

Cuno pulled the knife from Saber's gut, the hard case screaming and kicking his legs as a pool of dark blood formed beneath him. Cuno wiped the bloody blade on the hard case's jeans, and stood.

Saber stared up at him, sweat beading his forehead and upper lip, his face shrunken. He swallowed hard. His voice was a barely audible murmur. "Finish me, damnit."

Cuno looked down at the dying man. He stared at him, expressionless. His chest rose and fell. Slowly, he sheathed his bowie.

"Die slow," he said tightly.

He picked up the man's shotgun and tossed it several yards down the wash. He picked up the man's revolver and stuck it behind his belt, then turned and used his hands to lever himself up the ravine's lip.

Cuno barely heard the man's dying cry above the wind as he retrieved his rifle, jumped back into the ravine and up the other side, heading back toward the town.

In the church bell tower, O'Malley had sat down to rest his eyes a minute and had fallen asleep. He woke with a start two and half hours later, when the sun was a silvery smudge in the blowing eastern shadows.

Standing and gazing sheepishly at the town below, reorienting himself, he wondered if he'd missed anything. But then, he didn't remember hearing any gunfire. He considered returning to the saloon, and had nearly started through the trapdoor in the bell tower's floor, when a thought occurred to him.

Massey might have waited to show himself this morning.

O'Malley stood with his rifle in his arms, watching the town slowly swim into focus as the sun rose and the wind gradually died, the pelting grit losing much of its ferocity. The sky remained red with suspended desert dust.

Fifteen minutes passed. Then a half hour.

And then O'Malley began worrying about the gold. Hudson, Saber, and Wilks might've skipped out with it during the night.

Cursing, O'Malley stooped and reached for the metal ring in the trapdoor. Before he could get to it, the door exploded outward with a vicious boom, exploding again as it fell back against the floor, its wind slinging dust.

A man hurled out of the dark hole and brought a rifle to his shoulder, his lips stretched back from his teeth in an exasperated snarl.

O'Malley had been waiting all night for Massey, but he wouldn't have been much more surprised to see Lucifer himself exploding out of the earth, wielding a smoking pitchfork. He was so startled that he dropped his rifle and tumbled backward, his heavy frame hitting the floorboards making nearly as much noise as the trapdoor had done.

"Hey!" the big man cried, hat tumbling off his shaggy head. He used his feet to push himself back toward the wall, one hand moving toward the walnut-gripped revolver on his right thigh.

"Leave it," Massey growled as he took the last three steps up the ladder and stepped onto the tower's floor, his spurs chinging on the weathered wood.

"Why?" O'Malley said defiantly, red-faced with fear and anger. "You're gonna kill me anyways, ain't ye?"

Massey froze, sighting down the barrel of the rifle snugged up to his cheek. He stared into the big man's eyes, wanting to take his time. But he had two more men to deal with, and the sun was climbing.

With a savage grimace, he pulled the trigger, blowing a hole through O'Malley's right eye and slamming his head against the wall, his left eye staring skyward with glassy shock.

The big man stiffened, then suddenly slackened. His chin dropped to his chest, and he slid down the wall, revealing blood and gore on the wall behind him.

"Yeah, I'm gonna kill you anyway," came Massey's delayed response as he turned and descended the stairs.

At the door of the church, he gazed down

the street at the saloon. The wind was still blowing but had died considerably, and he could see the saloon clearly. The sun had risen, offering a wan, red glow through the grit still suspended in the sky.

There was no movement around the saloon, but he hadn't expected any. He'd scoured the town before glimpsing the big man in the church bell tower, and he now figured both Hudson and the other surviving member of the gang, Kenny Wilks, had to be inside the saloon.

Tipping his hat low, he ejected the spent shell from his rifle and jacked a fresh one in the breech. The spent jacket clattered tinnily as he pulled his hat brim low and ran across the street. He pulled up before the assay office and walked toward the saloon, the butt of his rifle snugged on his belt.

He passed the boot and hat shop and a dentist's office and pulled up before the drugstore, whose wide front porch, sitting catty-corner to the wide main street, was gray and weathered and full of holes. Leaning against a post, he regarded the saloon sitting across the side street, which was now merely a lot tufted with sage and cactus and mounded with sand.

Behind him, a shingle chain screeched in the wind.

The saloon was quiet. From this angle he could not see the front window, only the long, rectangular-shaped body of the building. There were no doors on the wall facing him. If he was going in, he'd have to enter either through the front door, the front window, or the back door. They'd probably be expecting him at the back door.

So he'd try the front. . . .

He trotted across the lot and pressed his back to the wall. He looked toward the rear. Seeing no one, he sidestepped toward the main street and slipped around the saloon's corner to the front boardwalk.

Pausing, he looked around. Deciding no one had seen him, he sidled along the front wall and slipped a glance through the front door. The glass, upon which LOST LADY SALOON had been faded nearly completely away by the sun, was discolored from smoke and sand. Cuno couldn't see through it.

He moved back behind the wall and considered his next move. Hudson had Marcella and the boy. The quicker Cuno got into the saloon and killed Hudson and Wilks, the better off they'd be. He'd wanted to torture Hudson, reminding the killer for a good long time what he'd done to July, but mostly he wanted him dead.

Getting Marcella and the boy killed would

not bring July back from the dead.

Cuno set his rifle against the building. This was a job for the Colt, which he shucked from his holster and gripped in his right hand, working the stiffness from the torn palm by squeezing the grips over and over.

Finally, he lifted the .45 to his chest, gave a resolute sigh, and sprang toward the door.

23

Lifting his right foot, Cuno thrust it forward, placing his boot just below the doorknob. The weathered latch gave easily, and splinters flew as the door swung inward and crashed against the wall with a bang and a screech of shattering glass.

Cuno bolted forward with such power he couldn't stop, even when he saw Marcella and the boy sitting before him, only a few feet from the door. Marcella jerked her head toward him and screamed. The boy flinched toward Cuno as well, wide-eyed with shock.

As Cuno plowed into Marcella and the boy, his eyes raked the room, seeing Hudson headed for the rear of the room with bulging saddlebags draped over his right shoulder. Wilks was there too, and the younger, smaller man also had bulging saddlebags hanging heavily off his frame.

Both men turned sharply as Cuno tumbled over Marcella and the boy, throwing them both to the floor in their chairs.

Hitting the floor on both elbows, he looked up desperately. Hudson and Wilks had turned full toward him, dropping their saddlebags and drawing their revolvers. Both men fired wild rounds, the slugs plunking into the floor before and behind Cuno.

Marcella and the boy were wailing and covering their heads. Cuno drew his own Colt and fired, dropping Wilks with his first shot and turning his gun on Hudson. He fired twice as Hudson dove behind a table, then heaved the table over on its side for a shield.

Hudson fired two more rounds, both slugs chewing chunks from the table. He scrambled onto his knees as Hudson rose from behind the table, both sets of saddlebags draped over his shoulders, and bolted through a back door, leaving the door standing wide behind him.

Still on his knees, Cuno hurriedly thumbed cartridges from his belt through the Colt's loading gate. Marcella and the boy lay behind him, still tied to their chairs as well as to each other.

"Cut me loose!" Marcella screamed.

Cuno thrust the Colt's gate home and gave the cylinder a spin. Impatiently glancing at the door through which Hudson had disappeared, he cursed and bolted toward Marcella and the boy, shucking his bowie from his belt sheath. Mindful of Hudson getting away, he chopped at the ropes.

"He have a horse back there?" he rasped.

"*Sí.* He and Wilks decided to skip out with the gold. They thought you gave up."

Cuno sneered. "Good."

When the rope gave, he sheathed the knife. Taking up the Colt again, he bolted through the door at the back of the room. He was across the narrow storage room in three strides. He paused at the outside door and turned his gaze to his right.

Hudson trotted a big dun away down the alley, trailing a saddled black horse over whose back hung the two sets of saddlebags.

"Come on, goddamnit, *come on!*" Hudson raged at the black horse, which was apparently not accustomed to being led. The horse held back and shook its head with defiance.

The rider headed for the saloon's corner at an angle, which told Cuno that in a few seconds he'd be passing before the saloon. Cuno fired one shot, then wheeled back through the storeroom. In a wink, he was sprinting across the saloon floor, nearly running into Marcella, who had been making a dash for the rear. He paused before the front windows just as Page Hudson appeared on the street, spurring his dun into a clumsy gallop slowed by the resisting packhorse.

Extending the Colt at the window, Cuno fired. The glass exploded outward with a tinny shriek. Together, the Colt's pops and the shattering glass echoed loudly around the saloon.

Tracking Hudson's progress from left to right before the window, Cuno emptied his cylinder in less than five seconds. When he lowered the gun, he peered through the smoke wafting around him, through the window around which now only shards of glass clung to the frame.

Outside, Hudson had released the pack-horse. Hanging low over his own mount's neck, he clung to the saddle horn as the horse ambled in a loose-footed trot across the street, turned sideways, and stopped.

Hudson sagged, then slowly dropped down the horse's right front shoulder. When the dun gave a start and trotted off, dragging its reins, Hudson climbed to his hands and knees in the street behind it, his hatless head hanging weakly.

His heart pounding with fury and antici-pation, Cuno opened his Colt's loading gate and plucked out the spent cartridges, which clattered to the floor and rolled. Quickly he began thumbing in fresh brass. As he did so, he moved to step through the broken window and head across the street for Hudson, who had fumbled over on his back, his chest rising and falling heavily.

A shot exploded behind Cuno. Excruciating pain seared his right leg, buckling his knee. He dropped, scowling, his brain reeling with confusion.

Turning, he saw Kenny Wilks lying chest-down on the floor, propped on one elbow. In the hand of that arm, his smoking revolver was pointed at Cuno. Wilks's pain-wracked face was red and sweat-streaked. He lowered the gun and awkwardly used both hands to thumb back the hammer for another shot.

Before he could raise the revolver, Cuno slammed his own gun's loading gate closed, raised the gun, and fired. Wilks's torso twisted back, his head whipping to the side, a bloody smear where his nose had been. The back of his head hit the floor, and he died with a bubbly sigh.

Cuno clutched his thigh and examined the wound. The bullet had entered through the back and exited the front. Bad, but not deadly. Quickly, he yanked off his neckerchief and knotted it around both blood-seeping holes in his thigh. His leg throbbed painfully, seemed to swell with prodded nerves, nauseating him.

As he finished tying the bandanna, he looked up. Marcella stood in the middle of the floor, watching. She watched not with sympathy but with a curious interest, her eyes dull with subtle cunning.

She was thinking of the gold, Cuno knew. She was thinking of Hudson lying out in the street, wounded.

"The others?" she asked Cuno, her voice husky with expectation.

"Dead."

He turned his gaze to the boy sitting on the floor, his back to the bar. The kid's face was bleached out beneath the dust streaks and pinkish clay caking his eyebrows. He looked as though the horror of the last few days had left him witless. No doubt he wished Cuno had let him take his chances with the Apaches.

Cuno turned to Marcella, and was about to speak when a shot exploded from the street, the slug slicing the air over Cuno's right shoulder and thumping into the wall above a dusty piano. Marcella gave a surprised cry and dropped to her knees, looking out the window behind Cuno.

"Damn, I thought he was finished," Cuno said of Hudson, scuttling around and inching his head just above the window's base, peering out.

Across the street, Hudson was holed up behind a horse trough in which tumbleweeds had collected. The sun was well up now. The wind had died even further, but occasional gusts blew thin, gauzy curtains along the street. The sky was as red as the sky in paintings of hell. It gave the buildings along the street an eerie, salmon hue.

Hudson's head appeared over the horse trough. He extended his pistol and fired. The slug whipped several inches over Cuno's head and thumped into the piano with a raucous twang of vibrating keys.

Cuno extended the Colt and fired four angry rounds. Each shot blew up dirt before the trough or buried itself in the trough itself.

"I know you're hit, Massey," called Hudson's voice from across the street. "Might as well give it up!"

Cuno's face bunched angrily. "I gotta feelin' you're worse off than I am." By the way Hudson had sagged on his horse, Cuno knew he'd taken the slug in his upper torso, maybe a lung.

Hudson's only reply was two more shots.

Cuno slumped against the wall. Then again, a firebrand like Hudson might've cheated the reaper.

Cuno was considering his options when Marcella crawled to him on her hands and knees, allowing her shirt to flap open, offering a good view of her lovely breasts.

She extended her right hand as her wide, brown eyes gazed into Cuno's. "Give me your gun. I will sneak around behind him."

Cuno shook his head once in the negative.

"You'll never get him in your condition," she said, an edge in her voice. "He will get away. . . ."

Cuno winced, scowled, holding the neckerchief firmly against his leg. He wanted Hudson for himself, but he knew the girl was right. In his condition, he wouldn't be able to get him. He couldn't put much weight on his leg. Better Marcella finish Hudson than let the bastard find a horse and get away.

Cuno depressed the Colt's hammer, flipped the gun around, and set it butt-forward in her hand. She gripped it, turned away, and started crawling toward the back door.

"I can read your mind, Marcella," Hudson called in a mocking tone. "It ain't gonna happen, girl!"

Marcella froze and looked at Cuno quizzically. Cuno stared at her. Hudson must have seen Marcella move toward Cuno and figured she was taking the gun.

Or maybe he just knew she'd do whatever she must to get the gold.

Marcella pressed her back against the wall, cursing.

"Tell you what," Hudson called again. "You kill Massey, I'll share the gold with you."

His Colt in her hand, Marcella was still gazing at Cuno. It was almost as though she hadn't heard. Her expression did not change. She didn't even blink.

Cuno glanced at the gun, then returned his gaze to hers. He smiled but said nothing.

"You got my word, Marcella," Hudson called. "Kill him, you get half the gold. I ain't hit real bad, but I ain't in any condition to double-cross you. You kill Massey and get me to a sawbones, you get half."

Marcella's gaze remained locked with Cuno's. Her eyes were deep and impenetrable. Her breasts hung between the open flaps of her blouse, sweat-damp and streaked with dust and sand. Her right hand squeezed the Colt's grips so tightly the knuckles turned white.

"You believe that," Cuno said through a wan smile, "I'll sell you water rights in Death Valley."

She sucked her perpetually sneering upper lip and swallowed, maintaining her stare.

Cuno knew she wasn't so much seeing him as the gold. She'd come this far. She was too close to give up now. Wounded, Cuno was useless to her. If she killed him, she'd be allying herself with Hudson . . . at least until she could kill him and take all the gold for herself.

"Come on, Marcella, kill the son of a bitch!" Hudson yelled. Cuno thought he detected a weakening of his voice, as though he were losing blood. "You get half. I promise! I'm gonna need help gettin' the gold out of the desert, and so will you!"

Slowly, Marcella raised the gun. Cuno's smile faded as he watched the barrel jerk slightly as she drew the hammer back, her eyes narrowing.

"I am sorry about this," she said. By her eyes, he could tell she meant it.

His muscles tensed. Staring into her eyes, he knew. She'd resigned herself, steeled herself with purpose. Meeting her gaze was like looking into the calm center of a very large and demonic storm.

"Just tell me you'll kill him," Cuno said evenly, "first chance you get."

She nodded as she stared at him down the barrel of his Colt. "First chance I get . . ."

Her sentence ended with a gun blast. Cuno's head slammed back against the wall with such force it scrambled his brains for a moment.

Bewildered, he felt a tight breath fill his lungs and leave, felt the throbbing ache in his thigh. His eyes were closed. He opened them and looked around, shock shooting through him.

Marcella lay sprawled on her right side, blood leaking from the hole just above her left ear. The gun was still in her hand, cocked. Her eyes were open, staring at the dusty puncheons.

Cuno looked up. The boy, Sandy, still sat with his back to the bar. He held a smoking gun in both hands — Wilks's gun — the butt resting on his upraised knees. A look of deep consternation wrinkled his forehead and buried his eyes far back in his skull. He worked his mouth, as though trying to say something, but no words escaped his lips.

Not far away lay Kenny Wilks.

"Thanks," Cuno said to the boy.

He'd barely voiced the sentiment when Hudson called from the street.

"I knew you'd come through, girl! I knew it!" There was a moment of silence. The wind funneled under the saloon's awning and through the windows, rattling the glass shards remaining in the frame.

"Marcella! Come on out here and give me a hand up."

Cuno looked at the boy again, gestured with his hand for Sandy to stay where he was. Reaching down, Cuno removed his revolver from Marcella's still-warm hand. Then, using both a nearby table and the wall, he heaved himself to his feet, cursing the pain in his palpitating leg.

Grimacing, Cuno made his way to the open front door.

"Marcella," Hudson called, his voice growing doubtful. "What's goin' on? You kill him?"

Cuno stepped into the doorway, straightening, ignoring the pain in his leg. Hudson was standing now too, in front of the horse trough, half bent forward with a hand to his bloody left side.

"Shit!" he snarled when he saw Cuno.

Awkwardly, he raised his gun. Cuno extended his own revolver and fired.

Hudson's gun spun out of his hand as he gave a surprised cry and whipped the appendage to his chest, clutching it with his left hand. Blood oozed between his fingers until both hands were a bloody mess.

Hudson cursed and snarled like a wounded dog.

His fevered gaze rose to Cuno, still standing in the saloon's open door, gun extended. Cuno's face was stony, his eyes cold and dark. Blood soaked his right jeans leg, but the pain had become a dull, nebulous ache.

His eye twitching nervously, Hudson glared at him. His voice was cautious, halting. "Okay now, Massey — I ain't armed." He sucked a panicked breath as the two white scars in his cheeks turned even whiter. "I'm an unarmed man!"

"My wife wasn't armed," Cuno said mildly.

He lowered his gun to his side. He'd opened the wound in that hand, but like that in his leg, he was only vaguely aware of it.

"Boy," he said to Sandy, turning his head to the side, "you stay put. Don't look at the street."

Cuno turned again to Hudson standing before the horse trough. The outlaw wrung his bloody hands together before his chest — a sand-caked, bloody visage wracked with pain and terror. He cast a furtive look at his gun, lying in the sand several feet away.

"Massey, come on now . . . you tracked me all the way out here 'cause of a woman?" Hudson was exasperated. "You plumb loco? There's plenty o' women in this old world!"

Colt still down by his thigh, Cuno

thumbed the hammer back and started slowly across the street, his spurs chinging softly in the sand.

"You're crazy as a peach-orchard boar!"

"Yes, I'm crazy," Cuno said, gritting the words out on a taut wire.

Hudson shaped a nervous grin. "You . . . you come on down to Mexico, Massey . . . there's plenty of girls down there. I'll show you around."

Still moving toward Hudson, his jaw a wedge, Cuno said, "When you killed my wife, you shoulda made sure you killed me too."

"You got your whole life ahead of you, boy. Listen to reason!"

"When you killed July, you killed everything that mattered." Cuno stopped, looming over the firebrand. "Except killing you."

Inside the saloon, Sandy Hilman listened to the conversation in the street. He sat huddled with his back to the bar, staring across the saloon at a dust-coated painting of a naked woman holding a yellow rose. It hung by one nail on the facing wall.

"M-Massey . . . now . . . I ain't armed, damnit!" Hudson cried in the street, his voice obscured by distance and wind.

A short silence. Grit blew through the broken windows and ticked against the floor.

Sandy Hilman felt his heart beating with slow insistence.

"No . . . no!" Hudson cried.

A gun popped.

Hudson's voice again, shrill with agony and exasperation: "Ah, ye crazy son of a bitch . . . !"

For a long time, Hudson moaned. Sobbing, he cursed Cuno, begged for his life.

The gun popped again, a savage snap, making Sandy jerk.

He kept his eyes on the painting. The woman looked a little like his mother, he thought. She had been killed by the Apaches.

He jerked when the gun popped again.

A guttural plea rose weakly from the street, so soft that Sandy could barely hear it. Then the gun popped again, followed by low, panting squeals like those of a whipped dog.

Again it popped, like a metronome. Again, Sandy gave a start.

Sandy stared at the woman.

He pressed his ears closed and stared as he felt the reverberating shots . . . again and again. . . .

Peter Brandvold was born and raised in North Dakota. He currently resides in Colorado. His website is www.peterbrandvold. com. You can drop him an E-mail at pgbrandvold@msn.com.